DOCTOR IN BONDAGE

Doctor In Bondage

by

Irene Lynn

Dales Large Print Books
Long Preston, North Yorkshire,
BD23 4ND, England.

British Library Cataloguing in Publication Data.

Lynn, Irene
    Doctor in bondage.

    A catalogue record of this book is
    available from the British Library

    ISBN   1-84262-441-5 pbk

First published in Great Britain in 1970 by Robert Hale Limited

Copyright © Irene Lynn 1970

The moral right of the author has been asserted

Published in Large Print 2006 by arrangement with
Robert Hale Ltd.

Dales Large Print is an imprint of Library Magna Books Ltd.

Printed and bound in Great Britain by
T.J. (International) Ltd., Cornwall, PL28 8RW

Chapter One

The September evening was dull and overcast, and there was a hint of rain as Helen Crandall stood at the window of the duty office in the Foxfield Nursing Home in Surrey and mused for a moment in the quiet period before taking over her night duty. Sister Denby, whom she was relieving, was bringing her paperwork up to date, and she sat at the desk, head lowered in concentration, while Helen let her mind have a last wandering fling before settling into the routine of the night. Her blue eyes were bright as she watched the first misty drops of rain spreading through the trees and over the lawns.

'You'll have some trouble with Mrs Pierce tonight, I expect,' Sister Denby said, looking up for a moment. She was a tall, heavily built woman of thirty-seven, and was nine years older than Helen. 'Doctor Lymann has seen her, and he said he would look in again later tonight, so watch out for him.'

'I will. And what about Mr Thomas?'

'He'll be all right now. He's responding to that new drug.'

'Good. He was ringing his bell every other minute last night. I just couldn't get on.'

'You'll see a big difference in him tonight.' Sister Denby smiled as she returned to her reports. 'Matron was through here just after seven, and she tells me Mr Fredericks has had his operation. If all goes well and there are no complications he will be in our care early next week.'

Helen nodded, her blue eyes shadowing a little. Joseph Fredericks was the founder of Foxfield Nursing Home, and he'd been ill for some months with an aggravating chest complaint. She liked the man, but disliked his younger wife, Julia, who was a frequent visitor to the Home. There was a lot of gossip about the place concerning Julia Fredericks and Russell Garett, one of the two doctors on the staff, and Helen had a crush on Russell Garett herself.

'That will mean Mrs Fredericks haunting the place, I suppose,' Sister Denby went on slowly. 'She'll be giving us a bad name if she isn't careful, the way she throws herself at Doctor Garett.'

'I don't think there's as much in it as they say,' Helen said hopefully.

'There's no smoke without fire, my girl,' Sister Denby replied heavily.

Rain began to patter against the window, and soon turned into a heavy drumming. Helen moved away across the office and stood by the door. She could hear someone coming along the corridor, and somewhere one of the nurses was talking in hushed tones. But the evening was deadly still, as usual, and the old house was a sounding board for echoes.

Helen felt a remoteness seize hold of her. It was always the same when anyone spoke of Julia Fredericks and Russell Garett in the same breath. She suppressed a sigh and tried to concentrate upon what Sister Denby was saying, but her mind was perverse, and she could see a picture of Russell Garett's handsome face in her mind's eye. It wasn't as if Russell was unfriendly towards her. He had a cheerful word for anyone on the staff, and the patients liked him. But he never displayed any emotion deeper than friendliness, and it hurt Helen to know that she was slipping into love with him and could do nothing about it. Already she was feeling uncomfortable in his company, and when she could not see him her thoughts were with him.

'Mrs Francis will have to be watched

carefully during the night, Helen,' Sister Denby said. 'She's running a temperature, and Doctor Lymann wants observation on her, every thirty minutes. But it's all down in the report. I'm ready to go, so if you'll sign the books I'll be on my way, and I'll see you in the morning.'

Helen nodded and approached the desk. The responsibility of the patients was signed over to her, and she mentally shook herself as Sister Denby departed. Duty was a stern mistress, and harsh upon anyone who approached it with less than complete concentration. She sat down at the desk and read through the reports and checked the treatments list. Her two night nurses would be arriving at any moment now to relieve their day-staff counterparts, and then Helen would think of making her first round. But she could not prevent her mind clinging to thoughts of Russell Garett, and it irritated her to know that she was unable to keep him at bay in the way she was accustomed. Whatever was happening inside her brain, she had no control over it, and she dreaded to think that in a few more weeks she might be suffering the sharp, intolerable pains of unrequited love.

Nurse Hudson was the first to arrive, a tall

slim blonde like Helen herself, but Nurse Hudson was only twenty-three, and a silent type who hardly communicated beyond the bounds of duty.

'Good evening, Sister!'

'Good evening, Nurse.' Helen glanced instinctively at her watch. 'Perhaps you'll relieve Nurse Kerwin. Have you seen Nurse Baxter?'

'Yes, Sister. She came in from seeing her boyfriend about twenty minutes ago. She shouldn't be long now.'

Helen nodded and returned to her paperwork as Nurse Hudson departed. Her mind was now beginning to accept the rigours of duty, and already she was planning the night's routine, although it wouldn't vary much from the scores of other nights she had worked here.

She had been at Foxfield almost two years, and loved the old place and the work being a Sister entailed. She got on well with all the staff and the patients, although the latter were constantly changing. Matron was Miss Rose Hanley, a tall, thin, greying woman who was dedicated to her work, and the other doctor on the staff, middle-aged Ellis Lymann, was a bachelor who could be relied on to do his duties with the minimum of fuss. It was Russell Garett who caused the upheavals in Helen's life, although he and the rest of the staff had no inkling of the facts. Helen was good at concealing her feelings. She had accepted that Russell didn't care about love and romance, for he never looked twice at any of the nurses. But Julia Fredericks, eleven years younger than her ailing, sixty-year old husband, had attracted Russell from the beginning, and he was often in her company, usually on the pretext of talking about her husband. That part of it hurt Helen more than she was prepared to admit, and her misery had been added to recently by the increase of gossip about Russell and Julia.

Footsteps sounding in the corridor alerted her, and she sighed as she put down her pen and looked towards the door. Nurse Baxter appeared, breathless and worried.

'Hope I'm not late, Sister,' the slim brunette gasped. 'Our car broke down just outside Godminster, and we had to wait ages for the R.A.C. man. It's a wonder I got back here at all this evening.'

'It could happen to anyone, Nurse,' Helen said easily. 'Go and relieve Nurse Arden, will you?'

'Yes. Sister!' There was relief in the girl's

12

tones, and Helen smiled as she watched her depart.

There were thirty-eight patients in Fox-field, some recuperating after surgery and others resting from illnesses. Joseph Freder-icks had planned to run part of the nursing home as a clinic, but his own failing health had put an end to that because he had to give up his work as a surgeon.

Helen found her mind drifting back to Russell and Julia, and she got to her feet, her full lips pulled into a thin line. It was getting so every spare moment was lost to musing about her personal feelings, and that was not her nature. She didn't like brooding. Usually she was carefree, with a great love for her work, and she took things as they came, happy with life and her position in it. Her parents lived on the south coast, not many miles distant, and she went home to see them once a month. Her father was a solicitor, and her background was such that she fitted well into this select nursing home.

Nurse Hudson appeared in the doorway, and her face was tense. 'Sister, it's Mr Wid-dows! He's insisting upon getting out of bed again. Will you come and stop him? He's beyond me.'

Helen left the office and hurried along the

corridor, with Nurse Hudson following. There was always a nucleus of patients who gave trouble to the staff, and Mr Widdows, recovering from brain surgery, was one of them. Helen entered his room to find the old man sitting on the edge of his bed.

'Mr Widdows, what is the meaning of this?' she demanded in severe tones.

'I'm getting out of here, Sister,' came the steady reply. 'I can't take this any more.'

'What's wrong with Foxfield?' Helen closed on him, putting a hand upon his shoulder.

'There's nothing wrong with the place! It's just that I've spent long enough on my back.'

'Surely the cure is rest! That's what Doctor Lymann told me.'

'He said I could get up for a spell each day. I want to get a breath of fresh air.'

'I'll talk to Doctor Lymann this evening when he makes his round,' Helen soothed. 'Get back into bed now and try to forget these impulses. You could put yourself back a very long way, and I'm sure you won't want to do that after such a marvellous recovery.'

'Perhaps you're right!' Widdows was a small man, bald and wrinkled. He got back into bed and Helen tucked him in.

'That's right. I'm glad you've got some sense, Mr Widdows. You're better than a lot

of the patients we handle. I can't do anything at all with some of them.'

'But remember to talk to the doctor about
me,' the old man said plaintively.

'Your name will be the first I shall mention
when Doctor comes,' Helen promised. She
turned away, smiling at Nurse Hudson, who
followed her from the room.

'I don't know how you do it, Sister,' Nurse
Hudson said. 'I couldn't do anything with
him. He was going out for a walk in the
grounds, and there was nothing going to stop
him.'

'Keep a close eye on him, and I'll talk to
Doctor Lymann when he comes,' Helen
promised. 'Now we'd better take up the
sedatives list and settle the patients down
for the night. Where is Nurse Baxter?'

'She's in the kitchen getting the drinks
ready.'

'Good. I'd better check with her, but first
I'd better look in on Mrs Pierce. We can
expect trouble with her, Sister Denby says.'

'I've already been in twice to her,' Nurse
Hudson said. 'She's never satisfied.'

'She's been gravely ill,' Helen said slowly.
'It's up to us to see that she gets everything
she wants. In the next week or two she will
make greater recovery, and then she'll be

15

more reasonable.'

Nurse Hudson went on her way and Helen paused for a moment, staring along the corridor but seeing nothing as her thoughts intruded once again into her consciousness.

'Are you going to see Mrs Pierce?' a voice said at her elbow, and Helen turned her head to find Doctor Lymann nearby. He was barely taller than she, and his greying hair had receded greatly at his temples.

'Oh, good evening, Doctor,' she replied. 'Yes, I'm about to see Mrs Pierce, and Sister Denby said you were calling to see her again. Is there any cause for worry?'

'About her condition?' He shook his head as he fell into step beside her. 'No, she's all right – coming nicely out of the wood. But she's depressed by something, and I'm contemplating putting her on a course of drugs to try and relieve the pressures. Is there anything you can tell me about her? What does she talk about? Is there anything she hates about us, or anything else?'

'She complains a great deal about everything around her,' Helen said slowly. 'But that's usual, of course, in a patient recovering from such a grave illness.'

'Sister Denby has told me about this.' He nodded, his pale blue eyes clouded with

16

thought. 'I've yet to meet her husband, but Sister Denby tells me Mrs Pierce is always worse after he visits her. Have you met him?'

'No, I've been on night duty ever since Mrs Pierce has been here. But I've heard the nurses talking about him. He was shouting at her one afternoon during the week.'

'Was he, indeed? Well perhaps that's the key to our problems. I think I'll have Mr Pierce in to see me. What does he do for a living, do you know?'

'He runs a large garage in Godminster.'

'Of course, I remember now. Well I'd better see Mr Pierce.' He paused at the door of Mrs Pierce's room. 'See that an appointment is made for it, will you, Sister?'

'Yes, Doctor!' Helen followed him into the room, and they advanced to the foot of the bed, both studying the gaunted face of the middle-aged woman in the bed.

Mrs Pierce was very thin, and looked severely ill. Her pale face had lost what little flesh had clothed it before her illness, and her eyes, dark and lustreless, stared unblinkingly at them.

'How are you feeling now, Mrs Pierce?' Lymann demanded gently. 'Did those pills I gave you do anything for you?'

'I don't feel any better,' came the slow

17

reply. 'I'm too restless. I don't think I shall ever be my old self again.'

'You're feeling like this because you're not giving yourself every chance to recover,' Lymann went on sternly. 'I have asked you repeatedly to tell me what it is that's worrying you. The longer you maintain this hostility towards the nursing staff the longer it will take you to get well. We're on your side, you know.' His tones gentled a little. 'It makes us happy to see patients getting well and saying farewell. The sooner we get you up on your feet the better for all concerned. Now tell me what it is that's worrying you.'

'It's nothing.' The woman compressed her thin lips, and Helen watched her closely, looking for signs beneath the hard exterior. But there was no expression in Mrs Pierce's dark eyes, and no sign of her wanting to co-operate.

'Very well, Mrs Pierce.' Doctor Lymann turned away, but paused when he reached the door. 'I shall be seeing your husband very shortly. Is there anything in particular you would like me to discuss with him?'

'No. There's no need to talk to Eric! He doesn't know, or care, about me.'

'That's an unkind thing to say, Mrs Pierce. I hear that your husband is here to see you every afternoon without exception. But if you don't wish me to talk to him then I won't. Are you sleeping well?'

'Only with a tablet, Doctor.'

Lymann nodded and departed, and Helen followed him closely. In the corridor they paused.

'I shall still want to see her husband, so make a note of the appointment, Sister,' he said. 'I must get to the bottom of this. Her recovery is being retarded by this unco-operative attitude of hers.'

'Very well, Doctor.' Helen started back towards the office, but he called to her. 'Have you heard that Mr Fredericks will be coming here sometime next week?' he demanded.

'Sister Denby told me. I hope he'll get well soon.'

'From what I hear he's lost the will to live!'

'Really! Surely he's not the type to give up like that!'

'There's been so much preying on his mind, Sister. It's a fact that the mental condition of the patient is vital to recovery. It isn't so widely recognized as it ought to be. But we're learning all the time, aren't we?'

'We are, Doctor! But what is it that's worrying him? He was very happy the last time I saw him. This place is the outcome of his life's dreams. It's going very well, isn't it?'

'So it is, and he has no complaint there.' Doctor Lymann pulled a face. 'His marriage was wrong, you know. He confided that to me just after he married. He made a mistake, and he'll never recover from it.'

'He knew his wife for years before he married her,' Helen said slowly.

'She was an extremely clever Surgical Sister, but as a wife she leaves much to be desired.' A confirmed bachelor, Lymann could not keep his personal prejudices out of his tones, and Helen prevented a smile touching her lips.

'I hope he'll recover from his operation,' she said slowly. 'I like him very much. He's a wonderful man.'

'I'll second that!' He nodded and moved away. 'He'll get the very best nursing here, anyway. That's one good thing about it. He instituted this place and set the high standards. Goodnight, Sister. You'll know where I am if I should be needed.'

'Yes, Doctor.' Helen's eyes were bright as she went back to the office. She was thinking of Julia Fredericks. The woman had spent a lot of time at the nursing home before her husband had gone into hospital. She always used the pretext of checking up

20

on some administration matter, for she helped run the business side of the home. But she always saw Russell Garett when she came, and Russell was the junior doctor and not likely to know the answers to the sort of questions Julia had.

But there was no way of letting Russell know her feelings for him. As far as he was concerned she didn't exist. She was a member of the staff, and he never looked twice at her. She often wondered about his life, for there were not many facts about him going the rounds. The nurses didn't know anything, and if they couldn't glean the details then no-one could. But Helen knew there was some blight upon his life, for he rarely smiled, and never seemed light-hearted. He was carrying a burden, and she wished there was some way of finding out about it and trying to diminish it.

The routine of the shift swung into its steady pace, and after the patients had been settled down for the night, with sleeping tablets and sedatives administered where required, and rooms darkened, Helen sent the nurses to supper. She made a complete round of the patients then, satisfying herself that all medicines had been given and that the patients were indeed ready for the night.

Stillness and silence closed in, and her feet made no sound upon the polished wooden floors. When the nurses returned she went herself to the big kitchen to the rear of the building and ate a small supper, chatting with the cook on duty, but keeping one eye upon the clock. The nights were fairly quiet, and they could more than cope with the demands made upon them, but Helen liked to be on hand at all times, and she soon went back to the office.

Night duty was totally different to day shift, and of the two Helen preferred working nights. They spent a month on one duty, changing on the First of each month, and it was surprising how quickly the months seemed to pass. With the summer holidays behind them, and still fairly fresh in their minds, the onset of Autumn, with Winter to follow, was not too much of a burden yet, but the bad weather was a barrier between them and the next Spring. Already the flower gardens were looking sorry for themselves, and the wide lawns were carpeted with fallen leaves. It was a dreary time of year as far as Nature was concerned, and Helen was finding a similar mood falling upon her slim shoulders.

The long hours through the night were

fairly quiet, and she always looked forward to the dawns, but even they were changing now. The birds sang as usual, but never so early as in June and July, and the nights were getting longer, with dawn arriving much later than in the three previous months. But just after dawn the world seemed to wake up, and the day shift would soon be arriving. There was much to do in the early hours, and the passage of time seemed to speed up considerably.

Helen saw that preparations for breakfast were in hand, and checked the patients. The nurses took round tea, and breakfast was served shortly after. But it was for the first doctor's round of the day that Helen awaited, for the night duty doctor was relieved at dawn by his colleague, and this morning it would be Russell Garett doing the round. She opened the cupboard door in the office and glanced at her face in the mirror hanging on the inside of the door. There was a smile upon her lips as she saw the brightness in her eyes, and already her heart was beginning to anticipate Russell's arrival. She had tried to control these symptoms when first they had started reacting, but now she took them as a matter of course, and did her uttermost to conceal them. Her love, still growing day by day, for Russell, was her own closely guarded secret, and she didn't want even Russell himself to know about it. It was a forlorn emotion, barred as it was by his attitude towards woman in general, and the fact that Julia Fredericks seemed to dominate him. But there was no way of eliminating it from her mind. Despite the obstacles, she was always filled with optimism that each new day would be the all-important one, when Russell would notice her, realize how lovely she was, and discover that he was in love with her.

But she realized that it was only a dream, and managed to keep it in its place. At times the knowledge made her feel melancholy, but her natural optimism made hope buoyant in her mind, and she could not remain forlorn for any length of time.

When Russell Garett appeared she was ready for him, and her blue eyes were filled with anticipation as he came into the office. He was tall, dark-haired and handsome, with brown eyes that were sharp and alert. At thirty, he was two years older than she, and he seemed to be everything that her dreams hoped for.

'Good morning, Sister,' he greeted formally, although they had known each other for quite some time. He had never been able to lose that stiffness, and she was beginning to think he was shy.

'Good morning, Doctor,' she replied, her face expressionless, her emotions well under control. 'It's going to be a nice day, isn't it?'

'Every day is a nice day,' he retorted, nodding. 'Anything unusual to report among the patients?'

'No.' She suppressed a sharp sigh. There was something unusual she would like to report, but she dared not. Watching his intent face as they began the round, Helen wondered what he would say if he knew about her love. He would be deeply shocked, in the least, and she felt a small desire to shock him with it, but managed to subdue it. The time wasn't ripe yet for any declaration, and she could only hope that some day it would be.

Chapter Two

Going off duty at the appointed time, Helen took breakfast, then went to bed. She slept until three in the afternoon, as a rule, and afterwards filled in her time by catching up on her work or going into Godminster to shop. There was very little relaxation in her life, except on those week-ends when she went home to her parents, but she loved her way of life, and the pressures did not worry her.

However she found it difficult to sleep on this particular morning, and after tossing and turning for two hours she got up and went to the window to peer out at the day. The rain had stopped, but there was a threatening atmosphere outside, and she shook her head and went back to bed. Summer had gone completely, and she was despondent because of it. Her brain was throbbing with thoughts of Russell Garett, and she went to the little dressing-table and sat down, staring at her reflection and shaking her head. Whatever had come over her? She was normally a well-balanced person, and had never been in love before. She had been concerned, at times, that love always seemed to pass her by, but now she had her share of it, and she didn't like the nagging tensions that filled her thoughts and interrupted and disturbed her orderly way of life.

It wouldn't have been so bad, she told herself, firmly settling down again with the intention of sleeping, if Russell knew of her feelings and could show some response. But as far as he was concerned nurses were not women underneath. She wondered if the intensity of her feelings could communicate itself to Russell when they were together. Sometimes she tried to exert some sort of mental power to convey her feelings subconsciously, but he never responded, and she was often disappointed. The fact that she was a Sister was also against her, for she led a very lonely life at the Home. The nurses had each other for company, but she was cut off from all human intercourse the moment she came off duty.

Eventually she slept, and awoke later than usual, with the feeling that something was going to happen that would be out of the ordinary. Anticipation thrilled through her as she dressed, and she determined to go into town, three miles away, and catch up on some shopping. There was a bus stop just outside the Home, and when she was ready she made her way there.

Waiting several minutes, she could not help hoping that Russell would appear in his car, going in the same direction, and she was disappointed when the bus arrived and she had to board it. She sat by herself, staring from the window as the bus made

27

the journey, and when she alighted in town and started through the crowded streets there was a loneliness in her heart that she could not shake off.

With her shopping done, Helen went into the restaurant above a large department store for a cup of coffee, and finding it crowded, moved towards a table where there was an empty seat. She was lost in thought as usual, and reaching the seat, glanced at the couple at the table as she sat down. She started in surprise when she found herself looking at Russell and Julia Fredericks.

'Oh!' Her surprise was complete, and she stared from one to the other, her small packages sliding from under her arm and falling to the floor.

'Sister Crandall,' Russell Garett said, smiling. 'Do sit down. It's rather crowded in here this afternoon, isn't it?'

'More than usual,' Helen said in confusion, but she sat down, set her coffee on the table, and bent to pick up her packages.

'I must be going now, Russell,' Julia Fredericks said, and glanced meaningfully at Helen. She was a tall, slim woman of forty-nine, and it wasn't until one was really close to her that signs of her age showed.

Helen felt her cheeks redden a little. 'I'm

sorry. I hope I haven't interrupted anything,' she said.

'Not at all.' Julia smiled thinly as their eyes met, and her dark eyes were filled with casual amusement. 'In fact you're a life-saver. If you're going back to Foxfield shortly perhaps Russell will give you a lift.'

'I shall be delighted,' Russell said instantly. 'If you must go now, Julia, then perhaps I shall see you soon. I'll think over what you've said, but I can't promise a decision in your favour.'

'I know it's asking a lot,' the woman replied, getting to her feet. 'But it's very important to me, Russell, so don't hurry your decision. Goodbye, Sister.'

'Goodbye, Mrs Fredericks,' Helen said, sipping her coffee.

Russell got to his feet, staring at the woman. 'I'll see you later, Julia,' he promised.

'I'll make sure you do,' came the departing retort, and Helen breathed a little easier when Russell sat down again at the table.

'You've finished your shopping, Sister?' he demanded.

'Yes, Doctor, but I'll catch a bus if you're wanting to get away. I'm in no hurry, but perhaps you are.'

'No.' He shook his head. 'I'm not in a

hurry. I'll get another cup of coffee and join you. Excuse me for a moment, please.'

Helen nodded, her heart beating a lot faster than normally. She watched him cross to the counter, and she had to take a deep breath in an attempt to control the fluttering emotions escaping from her control. She had dreamed of this moment for months, and now that it was here she could not really believe it. But reality was harsh, and thinking of Julia Fredericks, she knew she could not compete against her. They weren't in the same class, she told herself forlornly, and if the woman hadn't suggested that Russell drive her back to the Home he would have hurried out after her!

Russell came back to the table, and for a moment he sat stirring his coffee, his mind far from Helen, and she watched him with an ache in her heart. Then he looked up at her, and smiled thinly as their glances met.

'Sorry, I was miles away,' he apologized.

'How is Mr Fredericks today?' Helen asked, guessing that he had been to see the sick man, meeting Julia at the hospital.

'As well as can be expected, Sister,' came the slow reply. 'I think you'll be having him in your care within another week.'

'That's good news. I hope he'll continue

making progress.' Helen sipped her coffee, feeling just a little bit awkward. This was the first time she had ever come into contact with him off duty, and he seemed even younger in his casual clothes. But there was the same stiffness in his manner that was apparent when he dealt with patients, and Helen found herself liking him even more. If only he could lose that manner for a bit and show that he was just an ordinary man behind that professional mask!

'How do you like working at Foxfield, Sister?' he continued, and she had the impression that he was not really interested but asking just for the sake of having something to say.

'I like it very much,' she replied. 'I'm very happy there.'

'And so, I imagine, is everyone else,' he remarked. 'I like it myself, and that's saying something.'

'You don't seem very hard to please,' Helen ventured, and saw him smile.

'That's true, but there are other circumstances to be considered. I'm not trying to make myself out a special case, Sister, but there are other considerations.'

'Sometimes that's the case,' she said. 'I'm quite happy that my life is uncomplicated.'

He looked into her face with a searching stare, and she guessed he thought she was alluding to Julia Fredericks. Then he smiled faintly, and some of the tension went out of his expression.

'I've often wondered about you,' he confessed. 'You never have any social life, do you? You're a very beautiful woman, if I may say so, but I've never heard that you've been out with a man, at least, not while you've been at Foxfield.'

'I'm quite happy the way I am,' Helen replied, but deep inside her there was an insistent voice pressing her to give him the opportunity to remedy that defect in her life.

'Do you hate men?' There was a gentle smile on his face as he awaited her reply.

'No!' She spoke forcefully. 'Why do you ask? Is there something in my manner which suggests that I do?'

'No.' He shook his head. 'Although you're a pretty formidable person on duty. There's something about you that's difficult to explain. When ever I see you on duty I get the feeling that you're above the ordinary things of life. I've never heard you talking about any of the staff. You don't like gossip, the nurses say. I think any man wanting to become interested in you would be daunted before he got to know you.'

'You seem to have analysed me very deeply,' she remarked.

'I do that to all the staff when I'm on duty with nothing much to do,' he said with a grin that made him look quite boyish. 'But don't you find it a lonely life at the Home?'

'Very lonely at times,' she admitted.

'That's what I thought.' He leaned his elbows upon the little table. 'Why the devil don't you get out and about sometimes? It's a short life, you know.'

'I am aware of that.' There was an unsettled feeling in her breast, and she found that she was breathing heavily. 'But it's easier said than done, you know, Doctor.'

'I suppose so,' he replied doubtfully, 'although I wouldn't have thought that a girl as lovely as you would have any difficulty.'

'Well I seem to get along all right without the usual complications that attend a girl's ventures into romance,' Helen said with a smile. 'Perhaps I'm getting the better of the bargain.'

'Someone is losing a great deal; some man, I mean.'

She shrugged and finished, her coffee, and lifted her gaze to his face again to see that he was watching her intently. He finished his coffee and started to get to his feet.

'If you're ready I'll start back to the Home,' he said. 'I have to be there at five.'

'I'm ready,' she told him, and her legs were unsteady as she stood up.

'Let me take some of those parcels,' he told her, holding out his hands, and a wave of emotion swept through Helen as she felt the power of his nearness. Her hands trembled as their fingers touched. He took some of the packages, and Helen dropped the rest.

'I am sorry,' she said, as he bent to retrieve them.

'My fault,' he declared, straightening with all the packages in his capable hands. 'Let me carry them, and don't leave your hand-bag behind.'

'Oh dear! I seem to be at sixes and sevens this afternoon,' she explained as she turned to pick up her handbag.

'Perhaps it's because you're not accustomed to a male escort around you,' he declared.

She glanced quickly at him, and saw that he was smiling, and she nodded casually, although her heart and pulses were racing.

'That must be the reason,' she conceded. 'I shall have to try and remedy that.'

'You wouldn't have much trouble finding

someone,' he told her.

Helen walked ahead of him, and they left the crowded building and he took her along to where his car was parked. They drove from town, and Helen was silent, tongue-tied now with an awkwardness that was most disconcerting. Russell didn't seem talkative himself, and she glanced at him from time to time, seeing that his expression was closed, and she knew his mind was working over some problem. She wished time could stand still at this moment. Her thoughts were tremendous, and the fact that she was with him in his car filled her with a trembling excitement that tried to betray her. But all too soon they were approaching the Home, and she gave a little sigh of regret because her dream was ending all too fast.

'Well here we are, Sister,' Russell said formally, as he pulled up at the side of the house, where a small park contained several cars. 'I don't know how often you go into town, but there's no need for you to go to the inconvenience of waiting for a bus, then standing around in town until one brings you back. I go into town on quite a number of afternoons during the week, and if you let me know when you're going in I shall be happy to give you a lift.'

'That's very kind of you, Doctor,' she replied. 'But I wouldn't want to impose upon you.'

'It would be no trouble at all,' he insisted. 'Don't be so independent. Nothing will happen to you because you ride in my car.' He was watching her with veiled amusement in his eyes, and Helen caught her breath.

'I wasn't thinking of that,' she said quickly. 'I just don't like being a bother to anyone.'

'Well you won't be a bother to me, I assure you,' he retorted. 'In fact I could do with some company myself. I've been talking about you this afternoon, about you not getting out and about enough, but I'm in the same boat, really, so I haven't any room to talk. I don't think it would harm either of us if we went into town occasionally to do your shopping, and to have a cup of coffee together.'

'It sounds like a good idea,' she said boldly, and could not prevent a rush of colour to her cheeks. There was a weakness inside her that was both pleasant and confusing, and she wondered if she had the strength to get out of the car.

'All right.' He nodded. 'On the strength of that I shall ask you out to town on Friday afternoon. Will that be all right? It will give you a couple of days to get over this afternoon.' A smile touched his lips. 'Too much excitement puts colour into your cheeks, and that won't do around the Home, will it? You'll have the nurses wondering if you're in love.'

Helen gasped, and took a deep breath, her eyes showing great brightness, and he laughed and got out of the car, hurrying around to open her door for her. Helen alighted and stood beside him, and he bent and collected her packages for her, smiling as she took them.

'It wouldn't be a bad idea if you got a shopping bag. Trying to negotiate a bus trip loaded like that must demand a great amount of concentration, co-ordination and juggling skill.'

Helen laughed shakily, and agreed with him.

'Let me open that door for you,' he suggested, 'or we shall be picking up those packages for the third time.'

He came very close to her as he opened the side door, and their faces were only about a foot apart. He was slow in stepping back, and Helen could feel his magnetism drawing her as he looked into her blue eyes.

'You are a very beautiful girl,' he said

slowly. 'I just don't understand why someone hasn't snapped you up. Are all your male acquaintances blind, or something, or is there some hidden snag about you that I don't know about?'

'There's nothing wrong, as far as I know,' she replied, smiling. 'Thank you for being so very kind this afternoon.'

'It was nothing. The pleasure was all mine,' he retorted. 'But don't forget about Friday afternoon, will you? You sleep during the morning, don't you? What time are you usually ready to go to town?'

'Usually about three-thirty.'

'And you're back here on duty at eight,' he mused.

'Not this Friday,' she informed him. 'I have the week-end free.'

'Oh, and does that mean you're going to visit your parents this week-end?'

'No, that will be on my next free week-end.'

'Then perhaps we can extend our afternoon together into an evening as well! Does that idea appeal to you, or are you too set in your conventional ways to want to make any unexpected changes?'

'It sounds interesting to me,' she admitted, and there was a surge of emotion to her breast. This just had to be a dream, she told herself. In a moment she would awaken to find that it was almost time to go on night duty, but she tried to hang on to the moment, reluctant to return to her normally lonely self.

'All right. I'll stick my neck out and try to be the first man to take you out for an evening. I don't know your likes and dislikes, but we'll get together when you're on duty and talk about it. You're often alone in that office during the night, aren't you?'

'For quite long periods,' she admitted.

'I'll see you then. I'm on duty tonight. I'm pleased we bumped into each other this afternoon, Sister.' He paused, watching her intent face. 'I can't keep calling you Sister,' he went on. 'Your name is Helen, isn't it?'

'Yes!' She could hardly get the word out for the emotion constricting her throat.

'Then off duty I shall call you Helen, and my name is Russell.' He stepped aside for her then, and Helen took a grip upon her senses and entered the building. 'See you later, Helen,' he said, and closed the door from the outside. His footsteps receded briefly, sounding on the gravel, and Helen leaned against the inside of the door and heaved a long, long sigh.

Her legs were trembling, and felt as if they

didn't belong to her. One of her packages slipped to the floor, and when she bent to retrieve it all the others dropped from her trembling arms. She picked them up, stifling a great urge to giggle hysterically, and she went hurriedly up to her room on the top floor, trying to convince herself that she hadn't dreamed up the encounter.

It was wonderful! She sat down upon the foot of her bed and stared dreamily into the future. It had been in her before going out! She recalled the sense of anticipation that had been upon her when she awoke earlier. But could it really be true? She breathed deeply, trying to contain the wonderful sensations flooding her mind. She had been in Russell's company, and he had asked her to go out with him on Friday! She closed her eyes and sank back on to the bed, lost in a whirling wonder of dreams. If she awoke now to find that she had been dreaming she would die of disappointment! But Friday was such a long way off – two whole days after tonight's duty! Anything could happen to change his mind. She suddenly found herself in a frenzy of doubt, and clenched her hands as she tried to will the Fates to be kind to her. Just this once! If only she could go out with him for the afternoon and evening! It would be the most wonderful time of her whole life! But nothing must be permitted to spoil the occasion.

The rest of the afternoon fled swiftly, for she had lost her sense of time. After tea she changed into her uniform, and still the fluttering sensation of happy emotion stirred in her breast. There was a picture of his face in her mind, and she hugged herself as she tried to contain her feelings. She was in love with him and nothing could ever alter that! Perhaps he could sense the great emotions sweeping through her! She had tried often enough to project her feelings to him. She tried to recall every single word he had said to her, and now she could not wait to get on duty; to be there when he made his round. And he wanted to talk to her about Friday! For the first time in her life Helen was supremely happy.

At eight she went on duty, and Sister Denby seemed longer than usual to hand over. There were the usual comments about the patients, and Helen had to force herself to listen, although there was a list on the desk noting all the important things like special treatments and points to watch for during the night. There were three new admissions, and Sister Denby described them in minute detail. Helen forced herself to be patient. Russell wasn't likely to make his round until the Home settled down for the night and things were very much quieter.

'I hear you came back from town this afternoon with Doctor Garrett,' Sister Denby said at length. 'It's the first time he's ever shown any desire to see the staff off duty.'

'I met him in town,' Helen said slowly. 'He was with Mrs Fredericks – they had just come from the hospital, I think, and she suggested that he drove me back here.'

'Well it's a change of heart, anyway,' Sister Denby said. 'I hope now the nurses will settle down. There's been a great deal of speculation about Doctor Garett, as you know. Now I wonder why Mrs Fredericks pushed you at him? It isn't like her to give ground on a thing like that. He's not the first man she's been seeing since her marriage. Perhaps she's getting tired of Doctor Garett at last, and thinks you're a suitable method of withdrawing from his life. It will be a good thing for all concerned if that is the true situation. A scandal here would make a great deal of trouble. If you like your work here as much as I do, Helen, you'll see to it that our handsome doctor loses what interest he has in our director's wife. With

Mr Fredericks coming here to convalesce it could be awkward, you know.'

'I'm sure you're reading too much into the situation, Sister,' Helen said stiffly. 'I'm sure there's nothing between Doctor Garett and Mrs Fredericks. It's obvious that she will see something of the doctors here.'

'She isn't so friendly with Doctor Lymann,' Sister Denby said quickly, and with a smile. 'But never mind. Don't you go getting too deeply involved, Helen. Stay out of deep water if you can.'

'Now you're being dramatic!' Helen said, and was relieved when Sister Denby departed. But she was disturbed by what had been said. Thinking back to the afternoon, she could see now that Julia Fredericks had been on edge about something, and recalling the few words the woman had said before departing, she guessed that some sort of a crisis had arisen. How it affected Russell she had no way of knowing, and she cut off her thoughts as the desk telephone rang. Lifting the receiver, she gave her name.

'This is Julia Fredericks, Sister,' came the surprising reply. 'I won't mince matters! I've seen Doctor Garett since you left him this afternoon, and he's told me about his arrangements with you for Friday. I want to

43

tell you that he has a previous engagement with me for Friday, and he's just being awkward about it. Rather than have any complications arising, I want you to turn down his offer.'

'But I can't do that!' Helen said explosively.

'I think you can,' came the strong reply. 'If you want to go on working here, that is. Goodnight!'

The line went dead, and Helen sat back as she replaced the receiver. She stared into space, her mind in a turmoil, disappointment flaring through her as her dreams began to shrivel. This was what she had really feared. There was something between Russell and Mrs Fredericks, and the woman had no intention of letting him out of her grasp!

Chapter Three

For some moments Helen was so shocked she could not think straight, and she stared at the telephone as if she had never seen it before. Then she took a swift breath, and her anger began to burn. What right had that woman to threaten? What business of hers was it if Russell wanted to take her out? She had no legal claim upon him! The thought evaporated her anger, and Helen steadied herself. The threat had come because Mrs Fredericks was afraid of losing her control over Russell. But what control had she? Were they having an affair?

Helen did not like to think of that, and a shadow crossed her face as she tried to erase the thought. But it stuck with her despite her efforts, and her face was grim as she went about her duties. Surely it wasn't as serious as all that! A doctor had to be very careful where his private life was concerned. He really didn't have a private life! All his actions and doings were suspect, and he could not plead privacy before a disciplinary committee. A sigh shuddered through Helen, and she began to think that perhaps Mrs Fredericks was trying to scare her into staying away from Russell.

But she couldn't do that, even if she wanted to for the sake of peace and harmony. She was in love with Russell Garett to such an extent that she would risk everything to have the chance of loving him! The knowledge was cold and stark in her mind, and she knew in that illuminating moment that she would never be satisfied until Russell himself knew of her love. It didn't matter to her what the cost might be! She was beyond caring. The break that she had longed for had arrived, and nothing short of a national disaster would make her change her mind.

When Russell put in an appearance to make the last round of the day she had managed to control and contain her passions, and the only sign of her heightened feelings was a glint in her eyes. But she smiled as he paused in the doorway of the office, and despite steeling herself against feeling too much of her love, she experienced a wondrous thrill that was worth all the uneasiness she had been suffering.

'Hello, Sister,' he greeted. 'You're looking smart and efficient this evening, as always. How do you manage to look so capable? I wish I knew the secret. Even if I come down here in the small hours, you still manage to look as if you've only just come on duty. Don't you ever feel tired?'

'Of course,' Helen replied softly. 'I am human, you know.'

'I have had doubts about that in the past,' he confessed. 'But I'll never wonder again. I'm glad we had the chance of getting together this afternoon. We've worked here for some considerable time, and yet we're still like strangers. That isn't so good for morale, is it?'

'I'll take your word for it,' Helen replied. She was telling herself that now was the moment to tell him she could not see him on Friday. If she wanted to avoid all kinds of trouble and complications she would do just that right now, but she knew in the back of her mind that she would never have the strength of character to cut herself off from him. She would willingly risk all the threats just to have some time with him.

'Have we anything on the list to cause us worry tonight?' he asked, coming into the office and dropping into the seat placed beside the desk. He leaned forward, his elbows upon the edge of the desk, and his dark eyes were alive with cheerfulness. She had never seen him so animated before, and there was a catch in her breath as she wondered if perhaps the development between them might be responsible. Her heart started singing at the thought, and she clenched her hands to prevent her fingers trembling.

'Nothing to worry about,' she reported. 'Mrs Pierce is still complaining, but Doctor Lymann is scheduled to speak to her husband. It seems that there's some concealed worry on the woman's mind, and we can't get at it.'

'I've seen a report from Doctor Lymann,' he said. 'Mrs Pierce is worried about the usual things – her home and its contents, and that sort of thing. She's also a little afraid of her husband, although he says she has no reason to be. He's not a violent man and has never threatened or raised his hand to her.'

'Then there's nothing we can do to help her in that respect, is there?' she questioned.

'Unfortunately, no!' He shook his head. 'If her husband could reassure her it might help, but it's rather out of our hands. Is there anything else?'

'Nothing worth mentioning. We can handle everything else.'

'Fine!' He nodded slowly. 'Let's make the round together, shall we? Then perhaps we can have a cup of coffee together. I do want to talk to you.'

Helen nodded, aware that she was powerless to deny him anything. They went around the patients, and half the time she was unable to concentrate on what was going on. In what seemed a record time they were back in the office, and she sat down to make out her notes while he watched her. She could feel

48

the intensity of his gaze upon her, and shivered inwardly, filled with so many strange emotions that she didn't know how to cope with them. From time to time she lifted her eyes to his face, to see the brightness in his eyes and the animation on his features. All of this seemed too good to be true, she told herself remotely. Surely Julia Fredericks couldn't do anything to harm her happiness!

'Nearly through yet?' he demanded at length.

'Just about finished,' she replied. 'Must keep everything up to date.'

'Of course. That's the only way to be efficient. I must say you're the most efficient Sister I've ever come across, and I've seen several good examples in my time. Where do you get all your energy from? How do you manage to get every detail? I've never found you wanting in anything.'

'Put it down to good training,' she retorted pertly, and he grinned.

'I'll do that, and now there's nothing left to keep your attention from me let's have a heart to heart talk.'

'What about?' She was trying desperately hard to keep her expression formal. Her feelings were swamping inside her mind like floodwater against a broken sluice gate. She had loved him for so long! He had kept at a remote distance, but now the barriers were down between them, it seemed, and she could not hold herself in check much longer.

'Well let's make a start with Friday. You haven't changed your mind since we first talked about it, have you?'

She thought of Julia Fredericks and tightened her lips. Here was another chance to tell him she could not see him, but her heart was against the very thought of it. What could Julia do about this situation? Precious little! She sighed as she nodded.

'Nothing has changed since this afternoon,' she agreed. 'I am already looking forward to going out with you.'

'Well that's good news! We'll have to have a long discussion about where we shall go and what we'll do. I've been working very hard lately, and a break will do me the world of good. I'm sure you don't get away often enough.'

'I'm very easy to please,' she admitted. 'Anything that will suit you will be all right with me.'

'I can't believe it!' He was smiling cheerfully. 'Have I really found the perfect girlfriend? Are you someone who will be easily pleased? Won't there be any arguments about where to go and what to do?'

'You sound as if you've had some unfortunate experiences with your friends,' she said, and he laughed.

'Yes, that does give the game away,' he admitted. 'But luckily I've never been serious over any girl in my life.'

Helen nodded, cheered by his words. He wasn't serious over Julia Fredericks! That was worth knowing. She tried to push all thoughts of the woman out of her mind, but there was so much at stake in the situation that she could not blot out the worries that attempted to overpower the pleasures.

'I'll pick you up here at around three on Friday, shall I?' he asked. 'You'll need a good sleep after coming off duty on Thursday. Have you any shopping to do?'

'I won't bother on Friday if we're going out. I can do it on Saturday.'

'Of course, you're free all week-end.' He eyed her speculatively for a moment. 'I'd better not start talking about Saturday or Sunday, had I? You may not take to my company on Friday. But as we are both off duty all week-end we might as well get together. It would be silly for two people to spend the week-end alone when they could get some enjoyment in each other's company.'

Helen felt her senses react to his words. Her happiness was complete, apart from a small, nagging voice in the background of her mind warning her about Julia Fredericks, but she tried to overlook that. She didn't think the woman could do anything to harm her future.

'What part does Mrs Fredericks play in running the Home?' she asked.

Russell's face hardened momentarily, then relaxed. She could see that he didn't like the mention of the name. He shrugged a little, shaking his head, and his brown eyes held a gleam of some intangible emotion before he blinked.

'She doesn't do much of anything,' he retorted, speaking as if the subject was distasteful to him.

'Has she any power?'

'Power?' He looked at her with narrowed eyes. 'How do you mean?'

'Well, Mr Fredericks is the managing director, isn't he, with a board of directors? Where does Mrs Fredericks fit into the scheme of things? Didn't she take over when Mr Fredericks became ill?'

'To a limited extent.' He was still watching her closely. 'She doesn't like a lot of responsibility, so she hasn't worked very hard at her duties. She has rather neglected them, as a matter of fact. I've been trying to help with some of them, but there isn't much I can do.'

She nodded, wondering if that explained why he had been seeing so much of the woman recently. Gossip had it that there was an affair going on, but gossip could have made the wrong observations against the facts. Helen felt relief drift into her mind as she thought about it. Appearances were rarely what they seemed. She took a deep breath and stifled the following sigh. Her mind was becoming a little clearer. Now she could begin to understand why Julia Fredericks was trying to blackmail her into keeping away from Russell. If the woman had been sure of him it wouldn't have mattered to her what he did in his off-duty periods.

'Has Julia been saying anything to you?' he demanded harshly.

'No. I think this afternoon was the first time we ever spoke to each other outside of duty.'

'I see. She's a strange woman, you know. Sometimes I wonder what it is that makes her tick. I don't wonder that her husband is ill, the way she treats him.'

Some of the intimacy seemed to have gone

out of the atmosphere, and Helen watched his face intently as he got to his feet. She had the feeling that her mention of Julia Fredericks had thrown cold water into his face.

'Well I'm glad we've got our arrangements made,' he said, standing by the desk and looking down at her. 'You won't change your mind in the next two days, will you?'

'No.' Helen smiled gently as she shook her head. 'I'm not a girl like that.'

'Good. I knew I could rely upon you.' He glanced at his watch. 'I'd better be on my way now. Mustn't interrupt your routine too much. I'll be in my quarters if you should need me, Helen.'

She nodded, filled with sudden doubt. Was there something between him and Julia Fredericks? She earnestly hoped there was not. Any such complication would be too much to bear. Her feelings were deep and intense, and heartbreak awaited any disappointment that might come. She watched his tall figure as he departed, and the sound of his footsteps receding along the corridor held her attention until she could no longer hear him. Then she heaved a long sigh and tried to relax. But she didn't like the side issue of Julia Fredericks, and knew that the woman spelled trouble in one form or another.

But she was going out with Russell on Friday! The knowledge was so thrilling that everything else was blotted out of her mind. She didn't care about the consequences. No matter what happened afterwards, she would have that evening with Russell.

Routine prodded her, and she reluctantly pushed her personal thoughts into the back of her mind. Time seemed to have no bearing now upon her duty, and she was like a girl in a trance as she went about her tasks. She hummed to herself, and felt a spring in her step, and all the time there was a tussle in her mind between her thoughts of duty and the rioting fragments of pleasure that arose from her knowledge that love had seeped into her life and invaded her whole being.

Morning came, and with it a great tiredness. Helen went off duty, ate some breakfast, showered, then went to bed, and she slept soundly until two-thirty. When she awoke she dressed and went for a stroll in the grounds, ostensibly to get some air, but she was hoping that Russell would see her and join her. She walked through the woods at the rear of the large building, and came eventually to the small, round summer-house that stood under the trees.

This little haven had been a haunt of hers during the summer months, and such was her temperament that she could find plea-sure in it during the rain of Autumn and Spring. She liked nothing better than to stand in its shelter and watch the rain streaming down. It was a lonely spot, and she liked to be alone with her thoughts. But as she approached this afternoon, teased by the wind, preoccupied by her thoughts, she failed to notice two figures standing in the shadows in the house. It wasn't until she heard a woman's harsh voice that she realised she was not alone, and she looked up, startled as a fawn is disturbed by some strange sound. She saw Julia Fredericks in the summerhouse, and turned instantly and stepped behind a tree, only faintly hearing a man's voice make some reply, and her face flamed as she imagined it to be Russell.

For a moment indecision gripped Helen. She was out of sight of the summerhouse, but she could hear Julia's voice ranting on, and she imagined the woman was talking about Russell's date with her on Friday. She was torn by two desires. She wanted to hear what was being said, and she wanted to run away and get out of earshot before she heard too much. She could hear Julia's voice quite plainly, for it had a strange, penetrating quality, but the man's tones were subdued, unrecognisable.

'I won't be treated in this offhand manner,' Julia was saying, and Helen frowned. This sounded like a lovers' quarrel. 'I'm not going to stand by and watch all my plans come to nothing because you're getting greedy. I've planned a lot, and you stand to gain much, but if you persist in this attitude then I'll call the whole thing off. There are too many side issues as it is, and if anything should go wrong then I'll lose everything. I'm not going to listen to another word. If you don't like my terms as we arranged them then find yourself another position and leave here. There's no room for adjustment in this business. Take it or leave it.'

The man's reply was indistinct, and Helen strained her ears in an attempt to pick up his words. But the next instant Julia came bursting out of the summerhouse, her face ugly with anger. She hurried along the path that led back to the Home, and Helen ducked down to avoid being seen. Moving quickly, she managed to get behind the summerhouse, and she went on along the path as fast as she could, wanting to get out of the vicinity in case Russell should emerge from the little building and spot her.

There was a wave of nauseating emotion inside Helen as she struck blindly through the trees. What was wrong in Russell's life that he had to be a slave to Julia? What hold did that woman have upon him? She drew a deep breath and exhaled slowly, throwing off some of her tension, but the pressures in her mind and heart were very great, and she was unsettled as she went back to her quarters. There she sat upon her bed and tried to think out what had developed.

She was not interested in Julia's plans, whatever they might be, although she couldn't help wondering what the woman had schemed that would reward her so greatly. The fact that she could talk to Russell so boldly and with such mastery in her voice made a greater impact upon Helen. Whatever there was between them, Russell was like a slave and Julia was making the most of the situation.

Trying to clutch at her new-found happiness, Helen wondered what she could do to let Russell know how she felt about him. If she showed her feelings too soon she might scare him off. He had to be interested in her to ask her out in spite of his friendship with Julia. But if trouble loomed because of what he'd done then he might think better of his rashness and decide against going with her.

Helen found anticipation building up inside her. Friday was still a long way off. It was the day after tomorrow, but that could be half a lifetime in terms of human relationships. Impatience began to fill her, and she felt uncomfortably irritable as she prepared to go to tea. Her night duty was before her, like a dark barrier to the pleasures of the future.

She was leaving the dining-room when a call made her pause, and she turned to find Julia Fredericks coming towards her. A spasm of tension flipped through Helen, but she controlled it, and waited for the woman to reach her.

'I'd like to have a talk with you, Sister, if I may,' Julia said, her dark eyes showing harshness. 'Would you come along to my husband's office? We can have some privacy there.'

'Certainly.' Helen followed the woman back along the corridor, and she had a nasty feeling that she knew the subject that would come up. But she had no intention of knuckling under to this woman, despite the threat that had been uttered the evening before. They walked along to the administration suite in the building, and Helen took a deep breath as they entered the well furnished office that Joseph Fredericks used.

'Sit down!' Julia said brusquely, moving behind the large desk and dropping easily into the padded leather seat.

Helen moved across the office and sat down on a straight backed chair beside the tall window. She watched Julia with an intentness that stemmed from uneasiness.

'I spoke to you over the telephone yesterday,' Julia said without preamble. 'From what I've heard today you intend to disregard me.'

'I don't see what business it is of yours,' Helen said stoutly, determined not to be browbeaten.

'I don't expect you to see how it affects me,' came the steady reply. 'But it is my business, I can assure you. I have big plans for Doctor Garett, and it would spoil them if he became enamoured with one of the nursing staff.'

'I don't see that it will necessarily come to that,' Helen retorted. 'I've been asked out and I'm going out with him.'

'I mentioned something about your

position here,' Julia said harshly.

'The days when someone like you could use a threat like that are over,' Helen said, smiling thinly. 'There's no way in which you can get rid of me. My work is satisfactory, and I cannot be made redundant. You'll be wasting your time if you take that line with me.'

'So you are in love with Russell.'

'On what do you base your opinion?' Helen countered, still smiling, although she was tense inside.

'It's in your face as plain as can be. Well you're a fool, Sister Crandall. I've always admired you, and from what my husband has said of you I take it you're far above average where nursing Sisters are concerned. Despite what you say, there are ways one can use to get rid of an unwanted employee, and I know of them. I would hesitate to go to any extreme, but I warn you that unless you do as I ask then something will happen.'

'You have no claim upon Russell,' Helen said thinly. 'You're a married woman. I don't think you are contemplating divorce.'

'I don't need to. My husband is a very sick man, and the latest reports upon him are far from encouraging. If he should die then I would have a great deal to offer a man like

Russell. There's this place, for instance. Any doctor would give an eye to be the boss here.'

'I'm sure Russell isn't the kind of man to want success thrust upon him at such a price.'

'You think you know Russell very well, don't you?' There was a grim expression on Julia's face, and her brown eyes were filled with anger and bright determination. 'Well you are in for a few surprises, Sister. I think I can safely leave this situation to come to its own logical conclusion. As far as I'm concerned there is nothing further to be said. But between now and Friday you ought to consider the advantages of working with me. Matron will be leaving us shortly, and there will be a pleasant vacancy for someone smart enough to consider her future. I hardly need to tell you that my husband, if he lives, will listen to anything I care to whisper in his ear. He's come to rely upon me considerably in the past months. Do think it over, Sister, I implore you. It would be a tragedy if you lost everything here, and your career into the bargain.'

'There's nothing to think over, Mrs Fredericks,' Helen said tensely. 'I can assure you that nothing you've said here will sway me from my own inclinations. I have admired you in the past. It's a pity that you choose to put barriers between us.'

'Very well!' Julia got to her feet with an impatient motion. 'So it's to be war between us, Sister Crandall. I hope you know what you are doing. I can't afford to lose. That makes me a very bad enemy. I've never lived by the rules, and I'll certainly not fight by them. I have the feeling that you're going to be very sorry over this little affair.'

Helen made no reply, but she was tight-lipped as she turned and strode from the office. Now she knew where she stood!

Chapter Four

Helen became so emotional about the situation before going on duty that evening that she had to sit down and think over what had happened before she could resolve herself to wait and see what unfolded in the next day or so. It was a decision that strained her patience, but she was well trained, and discipline came to her aid as she went through the routine of her work. She tried to tell herself that she was being a fool to worry about Julia Fredericks. The woman couldn't have any power over Russell! She was married, and that fact alone curtailed most of her activities. If she saw Russell at all away from the Home then it would be on the pretext of receiving help in her additional duties, and the times when they could get together for that were limited.

Doctor Lymann was on duty that night, and when he made his round just after Helen took over from Sister Denby, Helen sensed that he was concerned about something. But she didn't know him well enough to question him about his personal life. He lived quietly enough, she knew, but even bachelors had their problems. When they finished the round he followed her into the office, and sat down in the chair by the desk.

'Anything wrong, Doctor?' Helen felt constrained to say.

'Does it show that much?' he countered with a wry grin. 'It's nothing personal, mind you. I'm a man who has lived without any worries – so far! But I've been talking to Mrs Fredericks. I don't like the sound of what she has to say about her husband.'

Helen tensed at the sound of the woman's name. But Lymann didn't notice anything.

He was intent upon his thoughts. Helen sat down at the desk and took up her pen, fiddling with it as she waited for his next words.

'It will be a great pity if we lose him,' Lymann went on.

'Will it affect the situation here?' Helen demanded. She paused, then added: 'I don't mean to sound selfish. Mr Fredericks' death will mean more to me than the fear of having to find another position.'

'I know what you mean,' Lymann said. 'But you needn't worry about that side of it. Nothing will change here. I've got that straight from the horse's mouth, so to speak. Mrs Fredericks has assured me that she will step fully into her husband's shoes and take over should anything happen to him. But it will be up to us when he arrives, won't it? We must do everything in our power to put him back on the road to full recovery.'

'We'll certainly do our best.' Helen was thinking vaguely about her talk with Mrs Fredericks. Perhaps the woman would be in a position to do something about her if she so wished! But she pushed the thought aside. It would have to be a good reason for getting rid of her! Helen knew that normally there was no room for complaint about her work, and she resolved that in future she would be nothing less than perfect in everything she did. That would limit Mrs Fredericks' area of scheming.

'I understand from Mrs Fredericks that one of the doctors here may take over the big office if anything happens to her husband. He would, of course, be answerable to the board, but they would give him a free hand in most things. I don't know what Russell Garett will make of it, but I shall be very happy to fill the position.'

'Will it go to the senior man?' Helen demanded.

'That I cannot say. I would get the job if it did, but of course there are other things to consider in a matter like this. It is a more complicated position than a similar post in commerce or industry. One has to have special qualifications, and although I'm sure my own list is pretty extensive, Russell is a very clever man.'

Helen nodded, her mind racing along the avenues of thought that were opened by his words. She was recalling what she had overheard by the summerhouse that afternoon. No wonder Julia had said that someone stood to make a great deal. She thought of Russell, and wondered if he was the kind of man who would have an affair just to get on in his own particular work. She didn't think he was. He had asked her out on Friday, against Julia's direct wishes, and that didn't seem to be the way a grasping man would act.

'Well I'll be on my way,' Lymann said, getting to his feet. 'I guess you know where I'll be if you should need me.'

'Yes, Doctor!' Helen got to her feet as he departed. She followed him out of the office, and went in one direction while he hurried away in the other.

Reaching the end of the corridor, Helen turned it abruptly, and pulled up short as a burly figure almost walked into her. She gasped and put out her hands to ward off a collision, and the man, in a long white coat, caught her by the shoulders and helped her retain her balance.

'Sorry, Sister, I didn't hear you coming,' he said, grinning.

'My fault, Ralph,' she replied quickly. 'I've been here long enough to know that one should give corners a wide berth. Is anything wrong? We hardly ever see you around at this time of the evening.'

'A new case arriving. Apparently no one this end knows about it. Things haven't been the same since Mr Fredericks went into hospital. His wife can't cope like he did, and she's getting plenty of help, it seems.' Ralph Simpson, the porter, was a tall, burly man of about thirty-five, and he kept his powerful hands upon Helen's shoulders as he spoke. 'Have you got a room ready for the patient?' he demanded.

'All the empty rooms are ready for patients,' Helen retorted. 'But I'll get the nurses to make the bed before the patient comes up.'

'He hasn't arrived yet, but should be here in about thirty minutes. His papers will be coming with him.'

'Very well. Bring him up as soon as he arrives, will you? I will have a room ready for him. You'll find me in my office.'

'Okay, Sister.' Simpson turned away, then paused and looked into her face. He was a handsome man in a swarthy way, with heavy cheeks and crinkly black hair. On more than one occasion he had tried to interest Helen in himself, but she had always turned him down, and there was something about him that she did not like. She couldn't put a finger upon it, but when in his company she felt distinctly uneasy, and her impressions were never far wide of the mark. 'What about you and I getting together some evening?' he asked. 'I know you keep on refusing me. I'm not a qualified man, but I've got a reputation for being good company.'

'No thank you, Ralph,' she replied.

'You're off duty this week-end,' he continued as if she hadn't refused him. 'We could have a good time on Friday. That's my day off.'

'Thank you, but I can't,' she insisted.

'Well you can't blame a man for trying,' he said, shrugging his heavy shoulders. 'You never seem to go far, Sister. I'd like to get to know you better.'

'Sorry, but I shall be busy on Friday.'

'Some other time then,' he returned instantly.

'I don't think so.' She shook her head.

'I don't understand a girl like you. You're very beautiful. How is it you can manage without a man around you?'

'It must be the work, Ralph.' Helen smiled and turned away. 'I'd better get to work on a room for the new admission.'

He hurried away and descended the stairs, and Helen walked back along the corridor, her mind already working on the duties she had to perform. She saw Nurse Hudson, and called to the girl, instructing her to prepare a room, and then she went on with her work, keeping her ears open for the first sounds of the patient's arrival.

Nurse Baxter came to look for her later, to warn her that the patient was being brought up, and as they left the office together Helen heard the hum of the elevator. They walked along the corridor and reached the elevator as the gates were opened. Nurse Baxter helped Ralph Simpson push the trolley along the corridor, and Helen took charge of the slightly built woman who came forward hesitantly from the lift.

'I'm Mrs Stilton,' the woman said. 'It's my husband you've got there.'

'I see, Mrs Stilton. Well you have nothing to worry about. Mr Stilton will be in very good hands here. Would you care to come along to my office and wait there until we've settled your husband into his room? Then you can see him.'

'Thank you, Sister. I hope he'll get on all right here. He's not out of the wood yet. He's had a major operation, and they had doubts that he would survive this long. But he is picking up a bit now.'

Helen nodded sympathetically, and led the woman back to her office, leaving her there and going on to the room to help get the patient into his bed. She found Mr Stilton to be an elderly man, very slight and very ill, and when he had been settled comfortably in his bed he opened his eyes and smiled up at her.

'How are you feeling, Mr Stilton?' Helen demanded. 'The trip hasn't upset you too much, has it?'

'No,' he replied faintly. 'I'm feeling fine.'

'Your wife is here, and she'll be coming to see you in a few minutes. But first I must get the doctor to see you.' Helen left Nurse Baxter with the patient, and saw Ralph Simpson back into the elevator. Then she went into the office to call Doctor Lymann, and he promised to come down immediately. Replacing the receiver, she smiled encouragingly at Mrs Stilton. 'You'll be able to see your husband as soon as the doctor has seen him,' she promised. 'I expect you would like a cup of tea, wouldn't you?'

'That's very kind of you, Sister. I wouldn't say no to that.'

'I'll get the nurse to bring you one, and I'll call you when you can see your husband.' Helen left the office, and met Doctor Lymann in the corridor. She accompanied him to the patient's room, and waited while he checked the man's condition.

71

'We'll soon have you up and about, Mr Stilton,' Lymann said cheerfully. 'It'll be much more cheerful here for you. I shall see you again. How have you been sleeping in hospital?'

'Not too badly,' came the whispered reply.

'I'll have a look at your papers and see what they can tell me, and tomorrow we'll see what can be done. Goodnight.'

Helen followed the doctor out, and they went along to the office where Mr Stilton's papers were lying on the desk. Lymann sat down at the desk, and Helen took Mrs Stilton along to see her husband.

When she returned Lymann was getting to his feet.

'No complications in this case,' he said. 'A month should see him up and about as of old. No treatment until tomorrow, Sister, but he can have a sleeping tablet if he finds it difficult to drop off in these strange surroundings.'

'Very good, Doctor,' Helen said, and walked with him to the stairs. After Lymann had gone she went on about her work, but as usual her mind was occupied mainly by the problems that confronted her.

It was the same during the next day, and she didn't see Russell again until she went on duty on Thursday evening. He came into the office just before it was time for his round, and Helen looked into his face and felt her heart miss a beat when she saw the worried expression he was wearing.

'Is anything wrong, Russell?' she demanded.

'There is, and it's very wrong,' he retorted. 'I don't think I shall be able to make it tomorrow.' He paused and watched her for reaction, and she must have shown her disappointment despite her efforts to control herself. He tut-tutted, and shook his head. 'It is a disappointment for you,' he said slowly. 'I can see that. I didn't know you were looking forward to it so much!'

'I won't deny that I was looking forward to it,' she said, and there was fire in her cheeks. She met his gaze squarely, and she knew something of her love was showing in her expression. This time she made no attempt to conceal it. His face hardened as he caught her mood, and he came around the desk as she got slowly to her feet.

'Helen, I'm sorry,' he said, and reached out and touched her shoulder. She stiffened under his fingers, trying hard to keep her control. 'Look, I can't disappoint you so much. I had no idea that you were so keen on the idea of going out with me. I'll see you as arranged.'

'But you said you wouldn't be able to make it,' she said slowly. 'If something has come up that's more important then I'll gladly wait until another time.'

'If I don't see you tomorrow then there won't ever be another time,' he retorted.

'I don't understand!' She spoke slowly, watching his face, noting his changing expression. 'What's wrong, Russell?'

There was a tap at the door, and Helen glanced up swiftly, to see Nurse Baxter standing there.

'Sister, I'm having trouble with Mrs Pierce,' the nurse reported. 'She won't take her sleeping tablet.'

'All right, Nurse. Leave her to me. I'll be along presently.'

Nurse Baxter nodded, glanced at the waiting Russell, and turned away. Helen tried to collect her scattered emotions. She looked at Russell again, wondering what was on his mind. He seemed ill at ease, and could hardly meet her gaze.

"What's wrong, Russell?' she repeated.

'Perhaps I shouldn't have made that date with you in the first place,' he said softly. 'I don't know what came over me that afternoon.' He paused and looked down into her face, and Helen felt a pang stab through her breast. Surely she wasn't going to lose him now! 'But I do know,' he went on slowly. 'I've had my eye on you for some time Helen. I've become increasingly aware of your presence. I've let my imagination and passions run away with me. But I've shut my eyes to a lot, and that was a mistake. I'm not really a free agent. I shouldn't have made that overture to you.'

'There's someone else in your life?' she faltered.

'Not in the way you may think.' His face was grim, his eyes narrowed, and Helen had to suppress the desire to throw herself into his arms. She watched him as if mesmerised, but there was a sinking sensation in her breast, and she could feel tears prickling behind her eyes.

'I'm not thinking anything at the moment,' she replied. 'I'm just puzzled.'

'I owe you an explanation.' He shook his head and sighed. 'But I don't think I'll do it now.'

She relaxed a little, feeling her legs beginning to tremble, and she was finding it difficult to keep her shoulders back. There was a lump in her throat and an ache in her heart.

'Has it anything to do with Mrs Fredericks?' she asked in strained tones.

'Julia!' The word snapped from his lips as if it were distasteful to him. 'What do you mean?'

'I don't know what I mean! But there is talk about you and Mrs Fredericks. I overheard her talking to you in the summerhouse in the grounds yesterday afternoon. I didn't eavesdrop intentionally, but she was almost shouting, and I couldn't help but hear every word.'

'You didn't hear her talking to me!' He seemed surprised, and Helen bit her lip. 'You heard her talking to a man in the summerhouse?'

'That's right. Have I made a mistake? I thought it was you.'

'Why should you think it was me?' His face was harshly set, and Helen thought he was angry with her. She made no reply, only lowered her gaze from his face, and he took her by the shoulders and held her firmly. 'Didn't you hear the man's voice?'

'Yes, I did. But he was talking in very low tones, and I couldn't recognise his voice. I naturally thought it was you. It's well known here that you and she are often together.'

'But only for business,' he protested.

'Someone has to help her run the place. She hasn't the brains to continue on the same level as her husband.'

'She spoke to me,' Helen said quietly.

His face lost some of its tension, and his eyes narrowed. He inhaled sharply, as if she had stuck a pin into him.

'What about?' he demanded.

'About you. She told me to make some excuse for not keeping that date with you tomorrow.'

'She did what?' There was disbelief in his dark eyes.

'It's the truth! She went further than that. She threatened to have my job if I didn't do as she wanted.'

'Well I'm damned!' He shook his head slowly, still trying to believe what she said.

'Would she have gone as far as that if you and she are on only a business footing?' Helen asked him.

'I don't blame you for being suspicious, and I'm sorry I've got you into this.' He spoke softly, quickly, as if ashamed that he had to apologise. 'You're such a wonderful girl, Helen. I've been longing to take you out for weeks. The other afternoon presented such a good opportunity of asking you, and I was overwhelmed when you agreed. But there are shadows in the background, and as you have guessed, it is Julia behind them.'

'What sort of a hold has she on you?' Helen shook her head. 'I just don't understand, Russell.'

'It's a long story.' He sighed again, heavily, despairingly. 'I'm an ambitious man, as you can imagine, and she offered a way up for me.'

'On what terms?'

'What do you mean?'

'She doesn't strike me as being a woman who would do someone a good turn without something in return.'

'You've got a good idea of what she's really like. I thought she was like that from the start, but I guess I didn't want to believe it. It was too late when I did find out to my own satisfaction. But don't let me forget this side issue. I thought I was the only one she was leading around by the nose. You say she was in the summerhouse yesterday afternoon, laying down the law to some man?'

'That's right. I'm sorry that I thought it was you. I didn't like to think it was, mind you, but from what I've seen around here it had to be you.'

'Well it wasn't!' There was a momentary gleam in his eyes, and then he smiled. 'But this is good news! She's probably adding more than one string to her bow. It might let me off the hook. I don't want advancement under her conditions. I'd much rather stay just as I am and get to know you better.'

Helen felt a warm glow start burning in her breast, and she took a deep breath. 'Do you really mean that?' she demanded.

'I wouldn't lie to you,' he said softly. 'I think too much of you to want to hurt you in any way.' He looked into her eyes, his hands still upon her shoulders, and Helen could not help swaying towards him. She heard his sharp intake of breath, and he glanced towards the door. 'Helen,' he said. 'I hope to God I've got one chance left to put matters right. I can't bear the thought of having to turn my back on you.'

She made no reply, completely dominated by his closeness. There was a tingling sensation in her breast, and her pulses were racing as if she had been injected with some powerful drug. Her only thought was that she loved him! He suddenly slid his hands off her shoulders and down her back, crushing her to his chest, and despite the sudden pang of alarm that someone might come along and catch them thus, Helen could not prevent her own reactions to his movement.

She put her arms around him and clung to him as if her life depended upon it. His mouth sought hers, brushing her cheek before fastening upon her lips, and she closed her eyes as the whole world seemed to riot. Her emotions were so intense there was a buzzing in her ears, and she thought for one heart-stopping moment that she was going to faint. Then sanity returned and she pushed against him, breaking away, breathless and incoherent.

'No, Russell! Someone might come! Please!' She hardly knew what she was saying. She felt confused and dishevelled, and her lips burned from the pressures of his mouth. She stared into his intent face, breast heaving, senses off balance, and her mind was filled with many strange sensations. 'Oh, Russell!' she exclaimed.

He seized her again, a half smile on his handsome face, and she did not resist him. A kind of madness seemed to take hold of her, a recklessness that betrayed her. But there was one remote thought in her mind. If Julia Fredericks wanted to remove her then the woman would never have a better opportunity than this very moment. If someone came to the office door and saw them locked in embrace, and talked about it! She dared not think of the consequences, and broke away from him again.

'Russell, no! Oh, please stay your distance!'

'Helen!' He was gasping. 'I love you! It's been in my mind for a long time. I don't know how I've managed to keep it in check all these weeks. But now the breach in your defences has been made. You can't deny it. You're in love with me.'

'I am, Russell! I love you!' The words were torn from her heart. Helen clung to him, unable to control her feelings. But there was a bitter-sweet sensation in her breast. He loved her! The knowledge was nothing short of miraculous, but there was Julia Fredericks in the background of her mind, and Helen knew the woman would not relent in any way. She had some strange hold over Russell, and would maintain it against all opposition. Helen tried to shut her mind to the awful possibilities of losing Russell. Surely his love for her would prove greater than any attraction Julia might hold out to him!

She looked up into his face, reluctantly drawing away from him and trying to induce some semblance of sanity to return to her. She was trembling, stirred by his kisses, moved by emotions she didn't know had existed in her. Hope struggled with despair in her mind, and she searched his intent face for signs of victory for herself, but all she saw were the same uncertainties mirrored in his dark eyes. He was in love with her, but he knew that outside factors, probably beyond his control, were present and immovable. In that moment, Helen didn't know whether to laugh or cry...

Chapter Five

Russell made his round, and Helen accompanied him, trying to regain her composure. There was a leaping happiness in her breast despite the worries that followed like vultures. She watched him as he chatted with the patients, or took pulses and temperatures. She could not define her love for him. It was all-consuming and all-embracing. Nothing else seemed to matter so long as she was able to remain at his side, to know that he loved her.

When they returned to her office he sat down beside the desk and waited for her to seat herself. She leaned her elbows on the desk and interlaced her fingers to stop her hands trembling.

'Feeling more normal now?' he demanded with a smile, and she nodded. Then his face sobered and set, and he stirred uneasily in his seat. 'What about tomorrow?' he went on. 'Do you want to go out with me?'

'More than anything in the world,' she retorted. 'It would be heavenly to get away from this place, to be able to focus my whole attention upon you.'

'Put it like that and I can't resist you,' he said. 'Would you mind if we met secretly, Helen?'

'Secretly?' she echoed in some surprise.

'Go out alone tomorrow afternoon, and meet me somewhere away from here.' He was watching her closely for reaction, and Helen had to try and blot out of her mind the rushing sense of disappointment. 'I'm sorry I have to ask this favour,' he went on. 'But it will be better than not seeing you at all.'

'Of course,' she said instantly. 'And am I to deny seeing you if someone should ask?'

He watched her face for a moment, no doubt trying to gauge the strength of her feelings. Then he nodded slowly, and she moistened her lips.

'All right. Where shall I meet you?'

'Catch the three o'clock bus into God-minster and I'll be waiting at the terminus for you.'

'I'll do that!' She spoke slowly, heavily. 'I don't pretend to understand what there is between you and Mrs Fredericks, Russell, and it isn't any of my business. But if she is helping you with your career then perhaps we ought to be a bit careful.'

'It's kind of you to look at it like that,' he said, and shook his head. 'But I have a feeling that Julia is leading me up the garden path. In view of what you've told me about that incident in the summerhouse I think I shall have to be very careful.'

'Doctor Lymann said something about Mrs Fredericks telling him that one of the doctors here would be taking over the Home if something should happen to her husband.'

'He told you that!' Russell sighed heavily, and there was some disbelief mingling with the surprise that filled him.

'Has she been telling you that you're the only candidate for that particular position?' Helen demanded.

'Something like that,' he said through his teeth. 'I'm beginning to see that I'm being taken for a fool.' He smiled thinly. 'I think I must be a fool for acting the way I have done. Even a child is known by his doings!' He laughed bitterly, and then got to his feet. 'But we'll come out on top, Helen, you'll see. I shall be at the terminus tomorrow in time to meet that bus. Will you be there?'

'I'll be there,' she promised.

He smiled gently and departed, and Helen sat back in her seat and listened to his footsteps receding. Her mind was filled with conjecture, mingled with hope and fear. What sort of a threat did Julia comprise? The woman had been very serious when she threatened Helen with dismissal, and she had hinted that she would have no scruples to get what she wanted. But then there had been the man in the summerhouse yesterday afternoon! Helen shook her head slowly. She didn't know what to make of it. She believed Russell when he said he hadn't been in the summerhouse. But the way Julia had spoken to the unknown man gave Helen the idea that someone was firmly under the woman's thumb.

She gave up wondering about it and went on with her duties, feeling happier as the night wore on. In the morning she would get to sleep as soon as possible, and when she awoke in the afternoon she would be near the time to meet Russell. She didn't like the idea of having to meet him secretly, but that would be better than not meeting him at all. From time to time during the night she paused in her work to consider the prospect, and her breast was filled with tremendous anticipation. Never had she experienced so many powerful emotions. It was amazing that a man could stir up so much in her! A few weeks ago she wouldn't have believed it possible, but then she had imagined herself to be deeply in love with Russell. She hadn't thought she could love him more, but the past few days had shown her that what she imagined to be the highest degree of love was only the beginning of something so powerful that it took her breath away to contemplate it. She raised a hand to her mouth, and could still feel the tingling imprint of his lips against hers. Fresh waves of love poured through her as she considered what had happened while she had been in his strong arms.

By morning she was returned almost to her normal level, but she knew her eyes were brighter than usual and her pulses seemed to be racing, as if she were about to come down with a fever. Nurse Baxter must have noticed her heightened emotions, for she remarked upon it when she came to report that the day nurses had arrived. Helen dismissed her quickly, and a few moments later Sister Denby appeared.

'Hello, Sister, going to have a nice week-end?' the older woman demanded as she sat down at the desk and took out her spectacles.

'Yes, I hope so,' Helen replied, and glanced at her watch, counting off the hours to the time she would meet Russell. She didn't think she would be able to sleep at all during the morning, but she had to try in order to be at her best later on.

'Are you going to see your parents this week-end?' Sister Denby persisted.

'No.' Helen shook her head, wishing her colleague would hurry up and take over in order that she might get away. Sister Denby nodded and went on with her work, and Helen stood still, waiting to be relieved, struggling to hold her impatience in check. When she was free to go she took a deep breath and hurried up to her quarters.

After breakfast she went to bed, lying in the curtained room with her eyes tightly closed, trying to find her tiredness in an attempt to beat the excitement that quivered in her breast. Several times she almost slipped into slumber, but at the crucial moment a stark thought darted into prominence in her mind and she would start a little and then try to commence the whole complicated sequence over again. But finally she drifted into sleep and knew no more until her little alarm clock called her back to reality.

Coming to herself by slow degrees, Helen was aware of a comfortable and pleasant sensation in her mind, and she stretched and yawned and tried to figure out what lay in store for her during the day. It was like waking up on a birthday and wondering what presents awaited her. Then she recalled that she was to meet Russell in town, and her sleepiness vanished and she leaped out of bed and prepared to get dressed. She took a shower and checked through her wardrobe. The afternoon was sunny, although the wind was blowing the leaves from the trees. Autumn was not quite upon them, although that certain despair was in the air, a kind of sulking on the part of nature because the bright days and the hot sunshine were gone for another year.

The time to catch her bus couldn't come quick enough for Helen, and as the last minutes ticked away she began to worry that something would come up to prevent her keeping the date. But she was at the bus stop when the vehicle appeared, and it soon carried her into Godminster. When it reached the terminus her heart gave a great leap, for Russell was standing to one side, waiting for her, and she alighted and ran up to him like any young girl on a first date.

'Helen,' he said quietly, staring into her face. 'How beautiful you are! I've been standing here in a sweat, wondering if you got away all right. Were there no last moment complications?'

'Nothing,' she confessed with a smile. 'I was worried about the same thing, and then I caught the bus and sat rigid all the way into town wondering if you would be here.'

'I'm glad to hear that you care as much about me,' he said, and put his arm around her shoulder. 'Come on, my car is just outside.'

'Where are we going?' She clung to his arm as they walked out to the street. This was the most wonderful afternoon of her life. Looking into his face, she could hardly believe her good fortune at being in his company. She had dreamed of this very thing many times during the lonely watches of the nights on duty. She took a long, shuddering breath of satisfaction, and held him tightly in case the whole thing should still be a dream and rob her of the pleasure now filling her.

'I thought I'd leave you to suggest some place to go,' he told her lightly. 'I don't mind for myself. I've got you away from the Home, and the whole week-end is ours to spend as we please.' He paused and looked down into her face, noting the happiness shining in her pale blue eyes. 'You are going to see me tomorrow and on Sunday, aren't you? It's a bit of luck our long week-end has coincided, and at this particular time. I don't think we ought to turn down this chance.'

'I'm not going to do anything to spoil this happiness,' she told him shyly, and he squeezed her arm and smiled gently.

'Let's go far from Godminster,' he suggested. 'I shall be on tenterhooks if we don't, because a certain person may be in town, and I wouldn't want to bump into her.'

'Take me where you will,' Helen said with a smile. 'I'm out for pleasure today, and nothing you do will disappoint me.'

He nodded and helped her into the car. Helen settled down, still feeling as if she were in a wonderful dream. Russell got in behind the wheel and drove away from the kerb, and as they left the town some of Helen's tension left her.

'It's a beautiful day for a drive,' Russell commented. He smiled as he looked at her. 'You don't know how long I've been planning this moment. Now it's arrived I can hardly believe it's true.'

'That's the way I'm feeling about it,' Helen admitted. She watched his profile as he concentrated upon his driving. 'It's strange that we've never managed to get together before.'

'Not really.' His lips twisted as she glanced at her. 'I was aware of you from the very first moment I saw you, but I'm afraid my mind was set on other things.'

'You mean you thought Mrs Fredericks would help you far more than falling in love with me.' Helen smiled gently.

'That sounds bad, but I suppose that's exactly what it was. I had some encouragement, mind you. Don't get me wrong! There was never anything between us! I'm a doctor, and I wouldn't take any kind of a risk, especially one of that nature. Apart from that I have the greatest respect for Joseph Fredericks.'

'I understand!' Helen nodded. 'But why is she so jealous about you?'

'I don't know.' He shook his head. 'That's

just the way she is, I suppose. She's always been talking about what she will do when she has full powers at the Home.'

'She's expecting her husband to die?'

'Yes. It seems the doctors at the hospital don't hold out much hope for him. He will be coming to us, and we'll know the full picture then, but there's not much chance for him.'

'And there's a mystery man in the picture somewhere,' Helen commented.

'The chap Julia was talking to in the summerhouse,' he said slowly, nodding. 'Yes. That was a surprise to me! I thought I was the only one being coached for the top position. But whom could it have been?'

'Doctor Lymann? He did mention that he hoped he would get the position. The fact that he knows about it proves Mrs Fredericks must have been talking to him.'

'That's possible, but I don't think he's the type to work that way. What was it exactly she said to this unknown man?'

Helen racked her brains for a moment, then gave him the gist of what she had overheard. He listened in silence, then shook his head again.

'You say there was a threatening note in her voice?'

'Yes. She was laying down the law to him, whoever he was. I was upset when I thought it was you, Russell.'

He smiled slowly. 'I'm glad it was someone else, because it lets me out. I'm not interested in the top job any more, Helen. I've come back to my senses, and all I want from life is you.'

She watched his face for some time, while he concentrated upon his driving. He seemed concerned about the incident, but she didn't see how it could really affect him, apart from freeing him from Julia's clutches. She was puzzled herself by the woman's choice of words to the stranger. What had Julia meant when she spoke of all the things she had done? What great plans had she made, and why did she need some unknown man to bring them to fruition?

'Has she ever asked you to do anything for her, Russell?' She spoke in musing tones, hardly aware that she uttered anything until he replied.

'What do you mean by anything?' he countered.

'I don't know.' Helen shook her head, irritated by her own vagueness. She sighed. 'Let's forget about it. We'll be lucky if she doesn't find out about this.'

'It's none of her business, although I would like to keep it quiet for a bit,' he retorted. 'But when it does get out I shall have a thing or two to say to Julia, don't you worry. She has no right to try and manipulate anyone's life.'

Helen tried to put all thoughts of the subject out of her mind, and she settled back to watch the road. Russell drove fast and Helen found great pleasure in just watching him.

'We could just drive,' he said at length. 'Do you like a car ride?'

'Yes. I'm easy to please. I've never been out in a car too often to make the experience boring.'

'Then I know just the place to go. We'll have tea at a little cafe in a small village that I know.' He glanced at her and smiled ruefully. 'It's about fifteen miles from my parents' home, but I daren't take you there in case Julia happens to ring my mother and word of our visit gets out. But I promise you it won't be long before we do go visiting together. Didn't you tell me your father is a solicitor?' He glanced at her, and Helen nodded. He nodded, too, and went on: 'My father is a doctor. Does that surprise you?'

'No.' She shook her head, and smiled gently. She could concentrate upon what he

94

was saying without losing the thread of her thoughts, and she was weaving a pretty picture in her mind. It concerned their future, and she didn't think it strange that she was considering important issues so soon. She felt that she had been in love with him for a very long time. They knew each other very well, and time now didn't enter into the process of cementing her feelings.

'He's a G.P.,' Russell went on. 'I could have followed in his footsteps quite easily. In fact he wanted me to go into practice with him as soon as I had qualified, but I had grander ideas, and that's why I was so open for someone like Julia.'

'Her name keeps cropping up in our conversations,' Helen observed. 'I do it as often as you. There's something about that woman I don't like. What is she trying to do? Does she really need all this additional help to see her through her work?'

'She makes out that she does,' he retorted drily. 'But I've come to realise that she's a very shrewd and calculating woman.'

'But what is she after?' Helen persisted. 'She's not doing it for the fun of the thing, is she?'

'No, I don't think she is! He shook his head slowly, still gazing ahead. 'But I don't know what she is up to. She hinted quite a lot at different things, but never came out into the open. It all seems to do with her husband, and she can't wait to get him into the Home for us to care for. She was a lot worse before he became really ill. Just lately she's eased off considerably.'

'And you don't know what's behind this interest in you, and this stranger you know nothing about?' Helen was trying to puzzle out what seemed like a mystery to her, but she had nothing to go on, and when Russell admitted that he had no idea what was in Julia's mind she dropped the subject.

They drove on until they came to a small village that was both picturesque and peaceful. A narrow street ran between two rows of old fashioned houses. There was one shop, a restaurant for the many sightseers who visited, and a small inn that looked as if it catered for the stagecoach trade. Helen was enamoured of the scene that confronted her as Russell halted the car on the cobblestones in front of the inn. He watched her expression as she looked around.

'No need to ask if you like this sort of thing,' he said. 'I can tell from your face. I'm glad you do like it, because I love anything like this. I make a practice of going around churches and old houses. There must be a great deal of sentiment in me.'

'I'm enchanted,' Helen said slowly as they alighted from the car. 'You couldn't have brought me to a better place, Russell.'

He took her arm, and she trembled at their contact. Helen glanced into his face, saw his affection and happiness, and was content. She knew nothing could detract from their association. He felt about her the way she felt about him. Each was conscious of the other's feelings, and both knew that this attraction between them was no ordinary emotion. Julia Fredericks and reality seemed far away as they entered the little restaurant.

Tea was a pleasure, and Helen found herself enrapt in what Russell had to tell her about her surroundings. He knew the history of the village, and enthralled her with anecdotes of the past. He had such a vivid way of expressing himself that everything seemed to come to life around her, and when they left the restaurant to go on a sightseeing walk around the place she was a little surprised and disappointed to see modern cars in the street and to know that nothing they did or said could bring back that peaceful past.

They looked in the church and paused by

the village green. The peacefulness tore at Helen's heartstrings. She was a great lover of the country. Then it began to rain, and they sheltered under a tree that was losing its leaves, and as raindrops splashed down through the sparse branches Russell took her into his arms and protected her from the worst of the weather.

'Helen, I love you,' he said slowly, his tones thick with emotion. 'All this seems just like a dream to me. I'm afraid to sleep at night in case I wake up in the morning to find it's all been a hopeless dream. To think that we've been working together all these months and never found the chance to get together! It's incredible! And now I shudder to think that I might never have got around to speaking to you. It was a chance in a million, you coming into town the other afternoon and seeing me in that restaurant.'

Helen nodded, agreeing with every word. She cuddled up to him, content, in this isolation, to be with him. She seemed to be elevated to the highest plane of happiness. It had never happened to her before, and the freshness and the power of her emotions were like wonderful dreams come true.

The rain came down with more determination, and Russell looked around for a better spot to shelter.

'Shall we make a run for it back to the street?' he demanded.

'No!' She spoke sharply. 'We're not getting too wet here. Let's stay a bit.'

'With pleasure!' His arms tightened around her, and she tilted her face for him to kiss. She closed her eyes and lost herself to the pleasures of fulfilled love, and time had no place in her heavens.

Later, when the rain eased and the shadows of approaching night were closing in around them, Russell suggested that they went back to the car. Helen agreed, and they had their arms around one another as they stepped out slowly along the road.

'I've never experienced a more pleasant evening,' Russell said slowly. 'What shall we do with ourselves over the week-end, Helen?'

'Anything you say,' she retorted instantly. 'Just so long as I am with you, I don't mind.'

'This is going to be a very nice association,' he went on. 'I haven't been in love before, Helen.'

'Neither have I!' She looked up into his face, and his eyes were gleaming. 'Can you be sure it's really love you feel for me?'

'I'm sure all right! One knows instinctively when it's the real thing.'

'That's how I think, but we must make sure, Russell.'

'We'll be sure!' He tightened his arm about her waist, and Helen laid her head against his shoulder. They went on in silence, each busy with the thoughts in their minds. When they reached his car, Helen waited for him to open her door for her, and she heard his muttered exclamation as he got into the car and leaned across to unlock the door.

'What's wrong?' she demanded, getting into the vehicle.

'This car parked beside us,' he retorted, pointing to his side. 'It belongs to the porter at the Home.'

'Ralph Simpson,' Helen said breathlessly. 'Yes, it does! I wonder what he's doing here?'

'Let's try and get away before he sees us,' Russell said urgently as he slammed his door.

'He must have seen your car when he parked,' Helen insisted.

'No doubt, but I don't think he'll be standing around waiting to find out what I'm doing here. Hold tight and we'll get away.'

Helen tightened her lips, her eyes searching the shadows as Russell backed the car on to the road. Then her heart seemed to miss a beat, for two people appeared from the inn and came towards the parked car. She recognised Ralph Simpson, and the girl with him was Nurse Baxter! They both looked with interest towards the car, and Helen turned away quickly, not wanting to be recognised.

'Did they get a look at you, Helen?' Russell demanded as he drove off.

'I don't know,' she replied slowly, and her fingers were crossed. But the incident had taken the edge from her happiness.

Chapter Six

The week-end proved to be the most exciting and rewarding that Helen had ever spent. Most of the time was passed in Russell's company, and they both recovered from the shock and gloom which had beset them upon seeing Ralph Simpson's car on Friday evening. Helen saw Nurse Baxter on Saturday morning before going out to meet Russell, and the girl never mentioned seeing Helen the evening before, so it was assumed that they hadn't been seen. Russell proved to be a most considerate and gentle man, and by the time the weekend was over Helen was completely lost to him. Her love knew no bounds. Her happiness was unlimited. Reality had lost its sharp edges, and the whole world seemed a different place. Even the weather had no effect upon her exalted mood, and although she was regretful when the time came for her to part from him on Sunday evening, the knowledge that there would be other happy times with him did much to soften her feelings.

'Goodnight, Helen,' he told her gently, sitting with her in his car in the park at the side of the Home. It was almost midnight, and Helen was tired, happily sleepy. He kissed her lightly, and she got out of the car. 'Next week is your last of night duty for a month, isn't it?' he continued.

'Yes!' She stifled a yawn, and watched his shadowed face with adoring eyes.

'Good. We'll be able to get out in the evening then. But I have a feeling that the next week is going to be an important one for us.'

'Why do you say that?' she demanded, pausing in the act of getting out of the car.

'Julia, Helen!' His tones sounded harsh. 'I've got to let her see that I'm of no further use to her. If she intends making trouble for you just because we've been out together then something has to be done about the situation. You'll take care, won't you?'

'Of course, but there's nothing she can do to harm me,' Helen told him firmly. 'I'm too good at my work to give her a chance of finding fault.'

'I know, but I also know Julia. If she threatened to find some way of getting rid of you then she'll do it.'

'I'll be careful,' Helen said. 'What do I do if she confronts me and taxes me about this week-end?'

'Tell her to mind her own business,' he replied, and smiled thinly.

'She wouldn't like that, but it sounds like a good answer.' Helen leaned sideways and kissed his cheek. 'I must go now. Goodnight, darling!'

'Goodnight, my love,' he replied, and caught hold of her and kissed her soundly.

Helen was reluctant to leave him, but eventually she got away, and went into the Home and up to her quarters. She could hardly keep her eyes open, and as she prepared for bed her mind was busy with all the impressions she had gained from the past three days. When she tumbled into bed her eyes closed instantly, and she fell asleep without trouble, although her mind was fairly alight with happiness and speculation. When morning came she was still exalted, and despite the rain beating against the windows, she felt that it was a wonderful day.

With the weekend behind her, Helen felt regretful during that Monday morning, and in the afternoon she went to bed in order to be ready for duty later that evening. Russell would be on duty that night, and with her feelings so powerful and sharp she could hardly wait to see him again. Yet she was a little apprehensive when she went on duty, and as soon as she took over she began to listen and look for Russell.

Nurse Baxter came into the office, and Helen watched the girl closely as they talked about the patients. She couldn't help wondering if her subordinate and the porter had seen her and Russell on Friday evening. Personally she hadn't worried a great deal about it, but Russell had seemed to be concerned, and Helen thought of that now as she spoke with the girl. But she didn't mention the subject and Nurse Baxter didn't broach it.

When the girl had departed Helen sat at her desk with a frown on her face, and she pictured Russell's face as she considered all that had been said about Julia Fredericks during the week-end. Taken as they had been spoken, the isolated fragments regarding the woman didn't amount to much, but adding them together brought Helen a much larger picture, and she couldn't help wondering what sort of a hold Julia had over Russell. Had he told her everything about his relationship with the woman? She began to doubt that he had, and this made her feel disappointed. But anything that detracted from her high feelings had to be shunned, and she resolutely tried to clear her mind.

The telephone rang and she answered it quickly, giving her name. She stiffened a little when Julia Fredericks spoke, for the woman's image was still powerful in her mind.

'So you decided to go against my wishes, Sister!' the woman said firmly. 'Well don't say you weren't warned. I'm greatly displeased with you. I don't know what you hope to gain by defying me, but I shall remember this incident, and if you know what's good for you then start looking for another position, somewhere far away from Foxfield.'

Helen gasped, stunned by what she heard, and she took a sharp breath in an attempt to bolster herself. Julia laughed harshly.

'I suppose you thought I was joking when I told you to stay away from Russell. Well you've made a mistake, and there's no way you can remedy it. Russell isn't for you. I have big plans for him.'

'It seems you have big plans for more than one man, Mrs Fredericks,' Helen said thinly.

'What do you mean by that?' There was a change of tone at the other end of the line.

'It doesn't matter. I don't know what you're planning, but you'd better leave Russell out of your reckoning. He won't go along with anything you suggest.'

'Is that so?' Julia laughed thinly, and the sound slashed across Helen's nerves like a blunt knife. 'So it's to be war between us! Well that's all right by me, because the way I'm made, I can take care of you. It won't be long before you're giving in your notice, Sister.'

The line went dead before Helen could summon up enough determination to reply, and she replaced her receiver slowly, staring at the instrument in a daze, wondering what was behind the woman's fierce manner. She stifled a sigh and shook her head. If Russell hadn't been completely honest with her in the past then he had some more explaining to do before very long, and she would be interested to know what was happening between him and Mrs Fredericks. But she could not get over the manner of the woman. Julia Fredericks was a deep-minded woman, and Helen knew the threats that had been made were completely genuine. She would have to be careful or she would be losing her job.

By the time Russell appeared she had decided not to tell him of her telephone conversation with Julia, and she watched his face closely as he sat down at the desk by her side.

'Hello, Helen.' His eyes were warm and gentle. 'How are you feeling after the weekend?'

'Regretful that it is all over,' she replied, smiling as she forced her harsh thoughts to the back of her mind. 'What about you?'

'Feeling much the same way, so it says a lot for our feelings for each other. But console yourself with the thought that there will be a lot more weekends like that one, and some even better.'

'Have you seen Mrs Fredericks?' She watched his face closely as she asked the question, and his eyelids flickered a little. He nodded slowly.

'Yes. I had a call from her this morning. I didn't tell her where I had been over the weekend, but she was curious. Has she been on to you?'

'No.' Helen didn't like telling the lie, but she needed time to consider what had been said, and if Russell knew about the conversation she'd had with Julia then he might want to have a showdown immediately. That could end in rather unfortunate circumstances for Helen, and she didn't want to take the risk of losing her job just yet.

'So the porter and the nurse couldn't have seen us on Friday evening,' Russell said in relieved tones. 'I was hoping it had been too dark inside the car for them to get a good look.' He sighed heavily. 'Let's do the round, Helen, then we can sit and talk. After having your company all weekend, I've missed you a great deal today.'

She nodded, and they left the office to make the round. But Helen was disturbed by what Julia Fredericks had said, and she could not keep her mind on her work. When they returned to the office they sat down, and Helen asked if Russell would like some coffee. He shook his head, watching her face closely, and she knew without doubt that he loved her as much as she loved him.

When he had to leave she walked with him to the stairs, and he took her hands and kissed her lightly on the lips. Helen looked around quickly to see that they were not overlooked, but the corridor was empty. She breathed deeply, gripped his hands tightly, and then let him go. He hurried away down the stairs, and Helen walked back slowly to the office.

Seeing Nurse Baxter in the annexe, Helen paused, then entered, and the girl looked up at her. Helen studied her face, wondering how to broach the subject nearest her heart. Nurse Baxter watched her in turn, and Helen had to say something.

'Did I see you out on Friday evening, Nurse?' she asked in pleasant tones.

'Yes, Sister. I saw you, but I didn't think you saw me.'

'I wasn't sure, and it wasn't until we were well on the road that it came to me it could have been you.'

'I didn't think you saw me.' Nurse Baxter was pleased at having been seen. 'I've been going out with Ralph for two weeks now.'

'Ralph! Do you mean our porter?'

'Yes, didn't you see him with me?' Nurse Baxter sounded a little surprised.

'No, I didn't.' Helen felt that a little white lie was justified. 'As I say, I didn't realise it was you until afterwards. It was getting dark then.'

'Yes. I wouldn't have seen you if Ralph hadn't told me it was Doctor Garett's car in front of the inn. We were inside. Ralph wanted to see who was with the doctor. Idle curiosity, I suppose.'

'Yes,' Helen said, smiling. 'I hope you had a nice time.'

'A wonderful time,' the girl retorted.

Helen went on her way, no clearer in her mind. How had Julia discovered that she had been out with Russell over the weekend? Had Nurse Baxter mentioned the fact, or Ralph Simpson, the porter? She didn't think so. Neither of them would have much opportunity of speaking to Julia. She went back to the office to check upon the treatments list, although she knew all the details by heart. But her mind was clouded by the mysteries that seemed apparent, and she could not keep her thoughts from them.

The night advanced, and Helen did an hourly round of the rooms to check the patients, moving silently and alertly. The nurses were always busy, but they didn't require a great deal of supervision. With two floors to take care of, one of the nurses was always on duty on the second floor, seated in an office similar to the one Helen used, and the second nurse shared her time between the two floors, as well as acting as a relief when it was time for a meal. They had tea three times during the night, made by one or the other of the nurses, and usually Helen came back from a round to find her tea on a tray on her desk.

Just after midnight Helen went up to the next floor, where Nurse Baxter was now on duty, and as she approached the top of the stairs she imagined she heard the sound of voices in low conversation. Frowning, she entered the corridor and paused, wondering if the nurse was having trouble with one of the patients, but there was no sound from any of the rooms, and Helen walked silently towards the office. The sound of voices was coming from the same direction, and there was a frown on Helen's face as she stepped into the doorway. She saw Nurse Baxter seated at the desk, and standing beside her was the porter. They both looked up at Helen, and there was a slightly guilty expression on the girl's face. But Ralph Simpson smiled a little, then moved away from the desk.

'Hello, Sister,' he said, nodding slowly. 'Just chatting up one of your nurses. Do you mind?'

'Not so long as it was business that

111

brought you here in the first place,' Helen told him.

'I brought up the clean laundry,' he said, putting out a hand and pointing to the large basket on the floor beside the desk.

'This is a strange time to bring it up,' Helen observed.

'I asked him to, Sister,' Nurse Baxter said, her brown eyes filled with sudden worry. 'I knew it came late this afternoon, and I wanted something to do to pass the time, so Ralph kindly brought it up for me.'

'I see.' Helen nodded, aware that Simpson was watching her closely with a grin upon his handsome but fleshy face. 'Is everything all right up here, Nurse?'

'Yes, Sister!' There was relief in the girl's tones.

Helen nodded and turned to go back to her own office. She glanced at her watch as she departed, and heard Simpson whisper something to the girl but couldn't catch what it was he said. The next moment he was hurrying along behind her, and when he came level with her he put out a hand and touched her elbow.

'I hope she won't get into trouble because I'm up here, Sister,' he said, staring boldly into her eyes.

'No, Ralph, I don't see why she should, but don't make a habit of coming up here when she's on duty. Your place is down on the ground floor, isn't it?'

'Yes, Sister, but it gets a bit lonely during the night. I go off duty at midnight, as you know, and I felt a little bit lonely. I wanted a chat before going to bed. You know how it is sometimes, don't you?'

Helen nodded and smiled, and they continued down to the first floor. She paused again as he stepped in front of her.

'I thought you were an understanding person,' he said lightly. 'I've been seeing something of Nurse Baxter off duty. I always thought you had no time for men, but I saw you out with Doctor Garett on Friday evening. You could have knocked me down with a feather. I've asked you out a lot of times, but you've never shown the slightest interest in me.'

'That's how it goes,' Helen said, watching his face intently.

'That makes it my hard luck, doesn't it?' He grinned again, but there was a hardness in his eyes that was not lost on Helen, and she wondered at it.

'Not that it matters at all, but have you told anyone what you saw on Friday?' she asked.

He smiled, and was a long time answering. When he did speak there was a different sound in his tones.

'Were you out with someone you shouldn't have been with?' he countered.

'Of course not, but we had arranged to keep it quiet for a bit. You know how people talk and make mountains out of molehills!'

'I do know. They've talked enough about me. But you don't like gossip or scandals, do you, Sister?'

'I'm not the type to listen or indulge in such things,' she retorted.

'That's what I've always liked about you.' He nodded slowly. 'But don't you worry. I haven't said anything to anyone, and I told Nurse Baxter not to mention that we'd seen you and the doctor together.'

'Your discretion is to be applauded,' Helen told him.

'I believe in the old saying; Live and let live!' He laughed quietly and turned away, and Helen watched him descending the stairs.

She was thoughtful on her way back to the office. There had always been something about Ralph Simpson she didn't like, and it was never more obvious than right now. But he had never said or done anything to give her cause to dislike him, and she couldn't really put a finger on the one point in his character that made him one of the few people she couldn't admire. Then she thought of the unknown man who had been in the summerhouse with Julia Fredericks on that particular afternoon, and she wondered if it could have been Ralph Simpson. After a little thought she dismissed the idea from her mind. Julia wouldn't have any dealings with a man like him. He would be beneath her, working as he did in his capacity of porter at the Home.

The days of the week passed by slowly, and Helen found herself filled with a sense of anticipation, waiting for whatever Julia was going to do to happen. But nothing happened, and Helen suffered a sense of anticlimax. When she saw Julia in the corridor the woman passed her with no comment, and it hurt Helen a little to be snubbed for no justifiable reason. But she consoled herself with the knowledge that she had Russell, and that was all that mattered.

On Thursday evening Helen went on duty to learn that Joseph Fredericks had been brought into the Home and was in a room on the top floor. Russell was on duty that night, and when he arrived to do his round

Helen questioned him about their sick boss.

'He's not so good, Helen.' Russell stared broodingly into her eyes. 'I don't think he'll ever get well again.'

'That's a great pity. He's a fine man!' Helen was sorry about the news, and her face showed her feelings.

'That chest complaint of his had him coughing harshly for years, Helen, and the physical effort has damaged the wall of his heart. I think it's only a matter of time for him, and Ellis Lymann is of the same opinion.'

'Does Julia know?'

'Not yet. Lymann asked me to tell her, but she's hardly speaking to me these days.'

'I'm sorry about that.' Helen watched his face intently.

'Why should you be sorry?' He smiled thinly.

'Because if you had kept away from me you would still be in her good books.' Helen shook her head sadly. 'You had a chance of getting somewhere with her behind you.'

'I'd rather have you at my side than Julia behind me,' he retorted. 'Don't let that worry you, Helen.' He paused and glanced towards the door as if afraid of being overheard. 'Has she ever said anything more to you about leaving here?'

'Those threats I told you about?' Helen shook her head decisively. 'No. I thought at the time they were just empty threats. There's nothing she can do about me, is there?'

'I wouldn't have thought so, but I do know her. Be careful that you don't give her any reason to find fault.'

'I won't. That's one thing you can be sure of.' Helen got to her feet. 'We'd better make that round now.'

'Surely!' He got up, and waited for her to reach his side. He touched her shoulder, and she looked up at him, to be kissed on the tip of her nose. 'This time last week we had a whole weekend stretching out before us,' he said regretfully. 'It's a pity that time passes so quickly when the good things are happening. It's one of the bitter facts of life.'

'Never mind, there will be plenty of other times, won't there?' she demanded. 'If you can't take me to your home yet, then why don't we visit my parents on our next free weekend?'

'That's a very good idea. We'd better find out if your parents like me.'

'I don't think we need worry about that!'

He nodded, and they left the office to

117

make the round. Helen was impatient to see Joseph Fredericks, and when they reached his room she found herself holding her breath as they entered. Russell opened the door for her, and stepped aside so that she could enter first, and she found herself looking into the intent face of Julia Fredericks as she crossed the threshold. The woman was seated on a chair beside the bed, and she was holding her husband's hand.

Helen had eyes only for the man in the bed, but she could not help feeling a pang of surprise at Julia's show of emotion. She had subconsciously looked upon the woman as being totally without feeling. But here she was, a dutiful and loving wife trying to give comfort to her very seriously ill husband.

Julia took her hand away from her husband's, and looked through Helen, who moved to the foot of the bed, her eyes upon the sick man's face. She was concerned to see how ill Joseph looked, for he had seemed the picture of health when they took him into hospital a month before. But surgery had pulled him down, and it was their job to try and build him up again into what he was before he had been stricken. She saw that he was asleep, and noted how the flesh had disappeared from his cheeks. He was pale and wasted, and his form under the bedclothes showed that the rest of his short body had suffered to the same degree. He was merely a shadow of his former self.

'He's sleeping peacefully, Russell,' Julia said quietly. 'You're not going to wake him now, are you?'

'Not if I can help it,' he replied, with a glance at Helen. 'I must take his pulse, of course. This is a routine that will take place every thirty minutes until further notice. He's so used to it, in fact, that he won't awaken if it's done gently.'

Julia got to her feet as Russell approached the bedside, and the woman confronted Helen. For a moment they stared into each other's eyes, and Helen could hear the hiss of Julia's harsh breathing. For herself, she had restrained her breathing, and could feel her heart thumping madly, although there was no cause for emotion.

'I want you to nurse my husband as you've never nursed anyone before in your life, Sister,' Julia said in undertones. 'If anything should happen to him because of failure on your part then I shall see to it that you never work as a nurse again.'

There was so much venom in the tones that Helen was taken aback, and could only stare at the woman as if she hadn't heard clearly what was said. Then Julia smiled grimly, and Helen exhaled sharply to rid herself of tension. So that was the slant of Julia's actions! If anything happened to her husband she would try to use the fact against Helen in an attempt to get rid of her.

Chapter Seven

Helen glanced at Russell, but he was on the other side of the bed. She made no comment on Julia's words, and walked around the bed to stand at Russell's side. She was stung by what Julia had said, and yet felt a little relieved to think that this was the best the woman could do to get rid of her. Russell apparently hadn't heard what Julia said, and he glanced at Helen, shaking his head slowly, his mind filled with concern for their patient. Helen had no intention of telling him what Julia had said to her. He signalled for her to go outside with him, and Julia followed him into the corridor, pushing Helen aside.

'I want to talk to you Russell,' the woman

said aggressively. 'Let's go down to my office.'

'I haven't finished my round yet,' he objected.

'My husband is your most important patient at the moment, and I want to discuss his condition.'

'I'm afraid you've got your values wrong, Julia,' he retorted. 'No patient here is more important than any other. Some of them are regarded as special, but only because of their condition. I am well aware that your husband is the founder of Foxfield, but that doesn't mean I can neglect the other patients to talk to you about him.'

'Very well!' There was a tension in Julia's voice that Helen had never heard before, and she glanced at the woman's face, seeing the vicious sparkle of anger in her brown eyes. Her full lips were pinched and cruel, and she seemed to be trembling with suppressed emotion. Helen couldn't help wondering what she was getting upset about. 'Perhaps you'll do me the honour of seeing me in the office when you've finished your round.'

'Certainly.' He nodded slowly, his eyes on her face, and then he glanced at Helen and smiled.

'Come along, Helen,' he said. 'Let's get on

121

with the round. How many more patients are there to see?'

'Nine,' Helen said softly.

Julia turned abruptly and walked away, her heels making a din on the polished floor. Russell stood watching her until she had turned the corner and started down the stairs. Then he glanced at Helen's set features.

'What was she whispering to you about in that room, Helen?' he demanded.

'Nothing much. She was talking about her husband's condition.'

He watched her face a moment longer before deciding that she had told him the truth. Then he lifted a hand to her shoulder and patted it gently.

'I love you, Helen,' he said firmly, and she imagined that he said it not so much for her sake but to convince himself, and she found herself wondering just what Julia had meant to him in the past.

'We'd better get on and see the rest of the patients before Julia gets really upset,' she commented.

'I don't care if Julia does get upset,' he said. 'She has no hold over me. I don't care if I lose the position I have here. I've been thinking it over, Helen. Perhaps it would he wise if I got out before anything happened. I could take up a partnership in my father's practice. He would love that!'

'Then I wouldn't see you,' she said.

'I've thought of that too! You could come along.'

'How? In what capacity?'

'We could find something for you to do. Father has a finger in the pie of a nursing home not far from where we live. Of course it isn't as large or as grand as this place, but you would love it, and we'd be near each other.'

'Let's talk about it some more when we're off duty,' she said eagerly. It seemed that a weight was lifting from her mind. 'If you're really serious about it then you'll find that I won't stand in the way of progress just because I may not want to move.'

'That's what I like about you.' He glanced along the corridor, then slipped an arm around her waist, pulling her close for a moment. 'I wish we were off duty,' he whispered in her ear.

'So do I, Russell.' She was worried that someone might see them. 'Don't think I don't enjoy being close to you, but I wish you wouldn't touch me while we are on duty. If one of the nurses saw you there would be trouble. No sense giving Julia some ammunition to fire at me. Remember that she has her knife into me.'

He nodded soberly. 'Sorry, my love. But all my principles go by the board when I'm near you. I can't help the way I act when you're around.'

She smiled as they went on, and when the round was finished she went back to the office and he went off to see Julia. Helen didn't envy him his job. What he had to tell Julia would make her realise there was more to her life than manipulating the male staff. She would get a shock, but somehow, Helen thought, it didn't seem in character for Julia to worry about anything, and that included her husband's health. She couldn't help wondering why Julia had married Joseph Fredericks. The founder of Foxfield was in his early sixties, and Julia was only about forty-nine, a vivacious woman who still maintained a great deal of her youthful bloom.

Russell came back later, just after Helen had sent Nurse Hudson for her meal. They each had a thirty-minute break for that, and with Nurse Baxter on the upper floor, Helen was more or less tied to her office in case one of the patients should ring for attention.

When she heard footsteps in the corridor she guessed it was Russell coming, but she wasn't prepared for the expression that was showing on his face when he walked in through the door. In a flash she thought that Julia had brought some pressure to bear upon him and that he was now about to reach some decision about not seeing her again. But she controlled her fears, and watched him intently as he sat down rather heavily in the seat beside the desk.

'What's the matter, Russell?' she demanded at length, when he didn't speak. 'It's not Julia again, is it?'

'What else?' He sighed deeply. 'I just don't know what to make of her. You know I went from here to see her in the office. I had to tell her that there was little hope of her husband making a good recovery. I thought she would be upset by the news, but I was shaken by her reaction. It wasn't what she said. She gave me all the conventional phrases, and they sounded like obscenities on her lips. But her eyes. I do believe she was secretly overjoyed that Joseph might die.'

'Russell!' Helen stared aghast at him. 'What are you saying?'

'I know it's a dreadful thing to put into words, Helen, but that is the impression she gave me.'

'Surely you're mistaken! I've believed for a long time that she is a very hard woman, but surely she has some feelings for her husband! She can't be without feelings. She was his Surgical Sister before they married. She was a nurse. No one without natural sympathy can ever make a success at nursing.'

'Our Julia is a very strange woman,' he retorted. 'I wouldn't have mentioned this to anyone but you. But I've been thinking quite a lot since I spoke to her and observed her reactions. All along she's been strange in certain ways. I think she's been hoping that Joseph would die ever since she married him.'

Helen shook her head slowly. She couldn't believe the woman was that bad. But she didn't know what made Julia tick. The woman was hard and secretive, passionate and self-centred. Joseph Fredericks had spoiled her during their short married life, and Julia wasn't one to let such habits change.

'I'd give a lot to know about that other man she's working on,' Russell said slowly. 'I don't think it was Lymann. He isn't the type to fall under Julia's spell.'

'More to the point, why does she want a

man in her power?' Helen demanded. 'She was working on you, Russel, but why?'

'I won't deny that she was, and I was a fool to go along with her. But she promised such a lot, Helen. I'm only human!' He smiled bitterly. 'But thank God I came to my senses in time.'

'Did she ever say what she wanted from you?' Helen waited for his reply with bated breath, half fearing that love was at the root of Julia's motives.

'No,' he said harshly. 'All I ever got from her was that in a little while I would be the doctor in charge here at Foxfield, and that the position wouldn't be the upper limit. I am ambitious, and I lost sight of the more general trends because Julia blinded me. But then my love for you proved too strong for her bonds, and I think I'm well and truly out of her clutches. I don't know how to explain it, but Julia has the ability to make a man feel enslaved to her. There was no physical attraction between us, but I always had the feeling that she could get inside my mind and command me against my will.'

'Well she's found someone else to fill your shoes,' Helen said, and there was relief in her tones. 'I feel sorry for him, whoever he is. But what if she decides to get rid of you now, Russell?'

'I don't think she will try that. But if she does it won't worry me. I have another string to my bow.'

Helen nodded, greatly relieved by his words. It seemed to her that Russell had escaped Julia's power. His love was strong enough to enable him to combat the woman's will. She recalled Julia's intense gaze, the blankness in the back of the dark eyes that shielded a sharp, calculating brain from the world. The woman had threatened to get rid of her because she stood in the way of some obscure desire. Helen shook her head as she contemplated. She would be surprised if Julia had any scruples at all.

'What about you, Helen?' he went on seriously, looking into her eyes. 'Has she said any more about getting rid of you?'

'No.' Helen found it easy to lie to him because she knew what he would do if she told the truth. 'But if she's found another man – that unknown fellow in the summer-house – then perhaps she won't be so keen to keep you on a string.'

He nodded, then smiled. 'That sounded bad, didn't it?' he demanded. 'But I suppose it was bad. This job is hard enough without a woman like Julia making it worse with her conditions.' He got to his feet. 'I'll be on my way, Helen. Keep a close eye on Joseph Fredericks, won't you?'

'I will,' she promised. 'Poor man! He's done so much to make this place what it is.'

Russell departed, and Helen sat for some time considering what he had said. Then she went on a round, and found that the nurses had changed duties and Nurse Baxter had gone to the dining-room for her meal.

Nurse Hudson sat in the upper office, and she got to her feet when Helen entered.

'All right, Nurse?' Helen demanded.

'Yes, Sister,' came the slow reply.

Helen glanced at her subordinate, but she was accustomed to the girl's quietness. Yet there was something in Nurse Hudson's manner that made Helen think the girl had something on her mind. She went to the chair beside the desk and sat down, her eyes on the girl.

'Something is worrying you, Nurse Hudson,' she said firmly. 'I know you well enough to recognise the signs. Is it something I can help with?'

'No, Sister. It isn't anything!'

Helen watched the other's face for a moment, then nodded. She got up again and walked to the door.

'Sister.' Nurse Hudson got to her feet and came around the desk as Helen turned.

'Yes?' Helen wouldn't prompt now. She waited for the girl to speak.

'Is it possible to lock the unoccupied rooms on this floor?'

'Lock them!' Helen was surprised by the girl's words. 'Why?'

'I don't know! Perhaps I'm being too nervous.'

'You've never been nervous in your life,' Helen retorted.

'Sometimes it's a bit creepy in the corridor with the lights down low and the silence pressing in as it does in the small hours,' the girl went on. 'I expect my nerves are a bit strained. But once or twice lately I've had the feeling that someone is around here.'

'I don't understand.'

'I found the door of one of the unoccupied rooms ajar last night,' Nurse Hudson said. 'The one right at the end of the corridor. I shut it, thinking it hadn't been securely closed, and when I came up to relieve Nurse Baxter about an hour later it was ajar again.'

'A faulty catch, I would say,' Helen told her. 'If you're starting to imagine things, Nurse, perhaps you'd better report sick and have a word with the doctor.'

'It isn't that,' the girl went on worriedly. 'I was afraid you would think that. Sometimes I think I've heard the sound of voices up here, when every patient is asleep and Nurse Baxter is alone in the office.'

'That sounds more serious,' Helen commented. 'Perhaps you are a little run down. Why don't you see the duty doctor in the morning?'

'I'm sure it isn't me,' the girl said. 'I closed the windows in all the unoccupied rooms the night before last, but when I checked before going off duty early in the morning next day I found one open a little.'

'Which room was this?' Helen demanded.

'The same one with the bad door catch. The one right at the end of the corridor, beyond Mr Fredericks' room.'

'Let's go and take a look at it, shall we?' Helen walked out into the corridor and Nurse Hudson followed her.

'I don't want you to get the wrong idea about me, Sister,' the girl said as they traversed the corridor. 'But for some time now I've been noticing these strange happenings.'

'Why didn't you report them immediately?'

'Because I thought you'd laugh at me!'

'I'm not laughing now!' Helen paused

131

when they reached the end of the corridor, and her heart seemed to miss a beat as she stared at the door of the room in question, for the door was ajar!

'There you are!' There was triumph and relief in Nurse Hudson's tones. 'The door is ajar now, and I checked it specially when Nurse Baxter went down on her break.'

Helen nodded and approached the door, pushing it open and reaching into the room to switch on the light. She peered around the room, which was empty save for the unmade bed against the right-hand wall, and turned to the nurse.

'There's nothing in here to be afraid of, Nurse,' she said. 'It must be the catch. Come into the room a moment.'

Nurse Hudson entered hesitantly, and Helen closed the door firmly. Then she pulled on the doorknob without twisting it, expecting the door to open, but it remained fast shut.

'There you are! There's nothing wrong with the sneck. I've tried that myself. The door doesn't open on its own. Someone is doing it deliberately.'

'Why should anyone want to do such a thing?' Helen demanded.

'I wish I knew.' Nurse Hudson looked

around the room. 'But at least the window is closed.'

Helen walked to the window and tested the catch. 'It's closed all right,' she said. Then she leaned forward and rubbed her hand against the white-painted sill. 'But this is wet. Have the windows been open at all?'

'I wouldn't think they'd been opened,' came the slow reply. 'I made sure they were shut when I came on duty at eight.'

'It hasn't rained today, but it was raining a short time ago.' Helen was concerned now. 'What do you think is at the back of these incidents, Nurse?'

'I daren't think about it, but I shall be very relieved when I go back on to day duty, Sister.'

'I'll have a word with Nurse Baxter when she comes back on duty,' Helen said firmly. 'Perhaps she can throw some light upon the matter. But you can go down on my floor and remain on duty there. I'll stay on this floor until Nurse Baxter gets back.' She turned and led the way to the door. 'By the way, has Nurse Baxter ever mentioned any incidents of a similar nature to you?'

'No, Sister. I haven't spoken to her about it, either.'

'All right, Nurse. I'll look into it.'

Nurse Hudson hurried away as fast as she could go, and Helen shook her head slowly as she left the room and securely closed the door. She pushed it without touching the handle, half expecting it to fly open, but it remained obdurately closed, and she stifled a sigh and went back to the office. She wondered about the incidents that Sister Hudson complained of, but could not find a reasonable explanation for their happening. The girl was obviously alarmed by them, and her nerves were suffering because of it. But before reporting the matter to a higher authority, Helen wanted to try and get to the bottom of it herself.

Some minutes later she heard the sound of soft footsteps in the corridor, and looked up expectantly. Next moment Nurse Baxter appeared in the doorway, and the girl paused in some surprise to see Helen seated at her desk in place of Nurse Hudson.

'It's all right, Nurse,' Helen said. 'There's nothing wrong. Nurse Hudson is down in my office. I want to talk to you. Come in and sit down for a moment.'

Nurse Baxter was strangely wary as she entered the office and sat down beside the desk. She didn't take her eyes off Helen's face, and Helen began to wonder what was causing the girl's alarm.

'Tell me, Nurse, have you ever noticed any strange happenings on this floor during the night?'

'Strange happenings?' The girl caught her breath, then gulped. 'What do you mean, Sister?'

'I don't know exactly.' For some obscure reason Helen didn't explain Nurse Hudson's fears. There was something in Nurse Baxter's expression which made her think the girl wasn't telling the truth. Was she like Nurse Hudson and afraid to voice her fears? 'I was just wondering if you had noticed anything unusual.'

'Something to do with the patients, Sister?'

'No. Obviously you haven't seen or heard anything or you would have said so. Forget it, Nurse. You're back on duty now, are you?'

'Yes, Sister. Is there anything you want me to do?'

'No. I see by your report that you're watching Mr Fredericks. There's no change in his condition.'

'I hope he'll get better,' Nurse Baxter said.

'And so do I!' Helen got to her feet and moved to the door. She glanced at her watch as she departed. 'I'll be up again at one a.m.

to check on his condition.'

Helen was thoughtful as she walked along the corridor, and she paused at the head of the stairs to glance towards the room at the far end of the passage. Considering Nurse Hudson's fears, she had to admit there was something in them, and resolved to keep an eye on the floor herself during the next duty or two. She went back to her own office, to find Nurse Hudson quite happy there, and she checked the list on the desk for injections, found there was none to be administered, and left the nurse to her domain, trying to quell her own restlessness with making another round of the patients.

Just before dawn Helen went back up to the floor above for the last time during her tour of duty, and she walked noiselessly along the corridor to the empty room at the end, to find the door ajar. She stared at it for a moment, frowning, remembering quite clearly that she had closed it firmly, and she recalled that this was exactly what Nurse Hudson was complaining about. It was eerie, she admitted to herself, and found her heart beating faster as she pushed the door wide then switched on the light inside the room. As she expected, the room was deserted, but she frowned as she entered to look around closely.

There was a little mark of water on the floor by the window, looking for all the world like part of the imprint of a shoe. She checked the window and found it locked, but she could not take her eyes off the tell-tale little mark. It could only have been made by the foot of someone who had climbed into the room through the window. There was a fire-escape outside the window; each corner room in the building had one, and Helen knew that rain had been falling through most of the night. She stood in the centre of the room for a few moments, lost in thought, and decided against taxing Nurse Baxter again. She knew she wouldn't learn anything from the girl. But she would keep watch the next night, and perhaps she would be able to discover just what was going on.

Leaving the room, she closed the door firmly, smiling thinly as she did so, and then went into the next room to look at Joseph Fredericks. She found him conscious, much to her surprise, and he smiled slowly as she reached the side of the bed.

'How are you feeling, Mr Fredericks?' she asked gently. 'Have you been awake long?'

'Not too long.' He said in laboured tones.

'Something awakened me, but I can't recall what it was. I've slept better than I did in hospital, however. There's nothing like being in your own place. I'm glad to see you still here, Sister Crandall.'

'It's good to see you here, Mr Fredericks,' she replied. 'Is there something I can get you?'

'No thank you. I'll just lie here until the day comes upon us. How have things been here while I've been away?'

'Much the same as usual,' Helen told him gently. 'We have more patients now than ever before. You've got quite a successful venture here.'

'I'm glad.' He nodded slowly. 'You go on about your duties, Sister. I'll be all right.'

She nodded and walked to the door, but he called to her as she was leaving, and she went back to his bedside.

'That patient next door,' he said. 'What's wrong with him? He was making a lot of noise. I remember now it was that which awoke me.'

'There's a woman patient next door,' Helen said.

'Not that side,' he retorted. 'In the end room. I heard his voice quite plainly. He laughed. Dreaming, I suppose. Anyway, not to worry. Perhaps I'll drop off again shortly.'

Helen nodded and turned away, and there was a coldness clutching at her breast. There it was again, she thought remotely. Nurse Hudson hadn't been imagining things. Joseph Fredericks' words proved that beyond all doubt, and Helen didn't know what to do about it.

Chapter Eight

That afternoon when Helen awoke she went in search of Russell, and found him walking through the grounds with a woman patient who had to get exercise. He paused when he saw her standing at the top of the path, then excused himself from the patient and came towards her, smiling as he reached her.

'Helen, it's nice to see you, but is anything wrong?'

'I don't know.' She was serious, and he quickly saw her mood. 'Can you spare me a few moments?'

'Certainly. Tell me all about it.'

She nodded, and gave him the details of what had happened in the corner room on the second floor. He listened intently, and his face was showing concern by the time she reached the end of her report.

'What do you think is happening?' he demanded.

'My first guess was that Nurse Baxter was seeing her boyfriend there when she knew the coast was clear.'

'The boyfriend being our porter, Ralph Simpson.' He nodded slowly. 'You say you found him in the office on that floor the other night?'

'Yes. He said he'd brought up the laundry. She said she asked him to because she had nothing else to do, and wanted to put the linen away in the cupboard.'

'And when you spoke to Nurse Baxter last night she denied all knowledge of anything unusual happening.'

'That's right. I didn't tell her exactly what the unusual happenings were, but she looked guilty. The thing is, Russell, what do I do about it now?'

'I'm not on duty tonight,' he said instantly. 'I'll keep watch on that room from the outside. I can stand in the potting shed to the side and see the fire escape. If it is Simpson I'll get hold of him and give him a good talking to. The damned fool knows the rules. It's bad enough having him sneak inside to see a nurse on duty, but when he wakes up the most important patient in the Home it's too bad!'

'I'll leave it in your hands then.' Helen was doubtful. 'I ought to put the details in my daily report, you know.'

'I know, and ordinarily I would tell you to do so. But if it is only Simpson then there's no need to make a big fuss about it. A few words in his ear should take care of it. If you reported it both he and Nurse Baxter would lose their jobs.'

'I know, and that's why I wanted to discuss it first with you. Will you let me know immediately tonight if you do learn anything?'

'At once,' he vowed.

She was relieved, and told him so, and he patted her shoulder and turned away. Helen watched him returning to the patient, and her heart was filled with joy. She could get pleasure just from looking at him! Then her frown returned and she walked along the path and back to the house. Going up to her room, she was filled with conjecture about the incidents taking place while she was on duty. The thought crossed her mind that if Julia learned of them she would place the blame fairly and squarely upon Helen's shoulders, and that might be sufficient to demand Helen's resignation! Helen's eyes narrowed as she considered it. She knew she couldn't be too careful.

By the time she went on duty that evening her nerves were as taut as Nurse Hudson's had been. She noticed it was raining outside, and hoped Russell wouldn't get wet or catch a chill from his vigil. She could hardly keep her mind on her duties, and several times during the evening she was tempted to tax Nurse Baxter about her suspicions. She said nothing to Nurse Hudson, and kept the girl on her floor, finding her plenty to do. When it was time for Nurse Baxter to go to the dining-hall Helen sent Nurse Hudson up to relieve the girl as usual, but with the knowledge that Helen would take over as soon as Nurse Baxter had gone.

Nurse Hudson insisted that she was all right this evening, but Helen was insistent, and a little later she went up to relieve the girl. Together they went to check the door of the end room, and Helen didn't know what to think when she found it closed tightly. But she sent Nurse Hudson below and waited out the time until Nurse Baxter returned.

Helen went back to her own office and let Nurse Hudson get away for her meal. But she couldn't settle down to anything. She paced the office and went along the corridor checking her patients. As time passed she became more concerned about Russell, and wondered how he was making out. She had barely returned to her office when she heard his footsteps in the corridor, and she was waiting at the door of the office when he appeared.

'No luck,' he said tiredly. 'I didn't see a thing. Have you anything to report?'

'I checked the door of the room and found it closed,' Helen said.

'Well that ties in. But what do you suppose happened? Did Nurse Baxter get nervous because of your questions? It's likely that she told Simpson to stay away for a few nights.'

'I didn't think of that,' Helen said slowly. 'But in future it will be easy to check upon Nurse Baxter's movements. I go up to the next floor at regular intervals, and they could time me almost to the minute. If I started going up at odd times they wouldn't dare run the risk of being caught by me.'

'It's a good idea, but I'd like to catch them in the act, if only to satisfy myself that Simpson is the cause of these incidents. Let's give it another night, Helen. I shall be

143

on duty tomorrow night.'

She nodded, content to let him take the initiative, and the rest of the night passed without incident. But she was still worried about it when she went off duty, and the uncertainties affected her sleep. She tossed and turned all through the day, and awoke earlier than usual, still wondering about the mysterious incidents.

Russell kept watch that next night, too, and nothing happened. Helen found that the door was now always closed, and so the nights passed and the weekend came and went, with nothing to disturb the peacefulness of the routine duty.

As the days went by it seemed that Joseph Fredericks rallied and began to make progress. Such was his improvement that by the end of the second week he was sitting up in bed and beginning to take an interest in his affairs. Helen saw more of Julia now, because the woman was always in her husband's room, either talking business or keeping him occupied with conversations of a more personal nature.

Helen found her subconscious fear subsiding. Julia did nothing to carry out her threats, and whenever she spoke to Russell, in Helen's company at least, there was always an aloofness in her tones that was unmistakable. Russell seemed easier in his own mind, as Helen was quick to notice, although he never spoke about Julia any more. When they were together Helen discovered the sweetest moments of her life. Never had she been so happy, or had imagined such happiness existed! Russell was everything to her, and she was eager for him to know it. Their love found its level and settled to it, and with each passing day Helen became more positive of her feelings and of what she wanted from the future.

Changing over from night to day duty meant that she could see Russell in the evenings, and Helen liked nothing better than a drive in the car through the lanes that were beginning to look bare and wistful. The leaves were nearly all gone from the trees and hedgerows, stripped by the fierce periods of high winds and driving rain, but she always felt so cosy inside the car, with her love burning brightly in her heart to keep her warm.

A month later Helen went back on night duty with her two nurses, and with so much time having passed uneventfully since their last tour of night duty, they were all content with the changeover. Russell was on duty that first night, and he sat in the office with Helen until almost midnight. They made a round of the patients just before ten, and then held a long discussion in the office about everything in general. At length Russell decided to go to bed, and Helen walked with him as far as the stairs.

When he had gone she went to the upper floor to check with Nurse Baxter, and was walking along the corridor towards the nurse's office when she heard a sound at her back. Turning quickly, she stared towards the end of the corridor, her mind trying to place the sound, and she thought she saw the end door closing. That room was still empty, and Joseph Fredericks was in the next room. For a moment Helen remained still, a little shocked, her mind overcome with unknown and nameless fears. Then she set her teeth into her bottom lip and hurried along the corridor to the room.

Reaching it, she paused and took a deep breath and then grasped the door handle and twisted it, sending the door wide with a sharp movement, reaching into the room instantly and switching on the light. Her breath escaped her with a rush as relief filled her, for the room was deserted. She had checked the room as soon as she came on duty, having made a habit of it since the night when Nurse Hudson first admitted her fears, and now Helen went forward to ensure that nothing had been touched since she had entered earlier. To her horror she found the catch on the window unfastened!

Helen stared at the window as if she had never seen it before. Then she reached out and pushed the catch home, wondering for an instant if she had made a mistake and forgot to check it. But she knew she had checked it. The window had been locked a few hours ago. She heaved a long sigh and glanced around the room before leaving, then went along to the office, her feet making no sound on the polished floor. She peered into the office before giving warning of her approach, and found Nurse Baxter engaged in writing up her report. For a moment Helen stared at the girl with her mind swamped with suspicion. Then she backed away and hurried back along the corridor, giving Nurse Baxter no clue to her presence. She went down to her office and sat down at the desk, aware that her legs were trembling. Then she telephoned Russell, sorry that she had to awaken him, but she wanted to talk to him, wanted to settle her own nerves before her fears had the chance to become firmly planted.

As soon as Russell heard what she had to say he agreed to come to her office, and she sat down at the desk and waited for him to arrive. He appeared some minutes later, looking tired and ill at ease, and questioned her closely about the incident. Then he nodded.

'It seems fairly straight-forward to me,' he said. 'I think it is Simpson sneaking in to see Nurse Baxter. She probably unlocks the window to let him in, and they stay in that room until he leaves. But you've closed the window again now, so he won't be able to get in.'

'I could swear that there was someone in that room when I went up to that floor. I heard a noise, and looked round quickly, and I'm certain I saw the door closing.'

'But you went straight to the room and opened the door,' Russell mused.

'That's right, and the room was empty.'

'Perhaps you surprised them. It might be a bit early for them. Now you've locked the window and Simpson won't be able to get in. I expect Nurse Baxter will check at any time. What's she going to think when she finds the window locked?'

'I don't know.' Helen shook her head. 'Do

you think she'll imagine she forgot to unlock it?'

'I doubt it. A girl in love wouldn't forget a thing like that. Would you?'

'No.'

'Well perhaps you can go up there and unlock that window again,' he said. 'Then I can set a trap for them. We must catch them red-handed in order to put a stop to it.'

'What will you do if you catch them?'

'Tell them to stop it. I won't let it go any further. But I can't let it go on. If Julia found out about it there would be the devil to pay.'

'But if Ralph Simpson was in that room and I scared him off he would have been on the fire escape when I locked the window. He might have seen me doing it. If I go back now to unlock it I'm sure he'll suspect that we're wise to what's going on.'

'Perhaps you're right.' Russell nodded slowly. 'That's deep thinking, Helen.' He smiled. 'Perhaps I'd better do this the hard way. I'll get a coat and go outside and keep watch for a bit. It's no use going up to the office. If Simpson is up there now we couldn't prove anything. He's on call every night. But if we found them alone together in an empty room I think it would be sufficient to admonish them. That should put a stop to them.'

'But you're tired, Russell,' she said. 'You need to get your sleep. I wish I hadn't called you now.'

'You did the right thing, Helen,' he told her, smiling gently. 'I spent some hours the last time you were on night duty in trying to put a stop to this. I shan't be satisfied until I do so.'

'All right. But don't stay out there too long. Is there anything I can do?'

'No. If I do see anything I'll come for you as a witness. If you stick to your normal routines you won't alarm anybody and make them suspicious.'

She nodded, worried now, and he departed hurriedly. Helen went back to her work, but her thoughts were with Russell, and the time seemed to drag. But within twenty minutes he was back again, his face grim and his eyes showing excitement.

'Come on,' he said quickly. 'I've just seen a man climbing into that end room. Nurse Baxter was at the window. Let's go up there and surprise them.'

Helen caught her breath, but followed him from the office, and she was aware that her heart was pounding painfully as they went to the upper floor, moving silently and quickly.

At the top of the stairs Russell paused and peered furtively into the corridor. Then he eased back and looked at Helen.

'The door of that end room is ajar,' he whispered. 'There's no light in the room. They'll see us if we walk down there.'

'What can we do?' Helen demanded. 'Won't it be sufficient to find them in there together?'

'Perhaps not. They could think of a reason or two why they should be in there together.' He sighed. 'I'll tell you what I'll do. I'll go up the fire escape and enter by the window. Simpson won't be able to make a run for it if I bar his way. You stay here and watch the corridor. I'll let you know when I'm in the room.'

Helen nodded, although she didn't like it, and Russell patted her shoulder and hurried away. When he had gone the silence in the corridor seemed to take her by the throat, and she gulped nervously. She did not look into the corridor in case she was spotted, but her ears were strained for the slightest sound, and suddenly she heard a smothered gasp. Peering into the corridor, she saw the door of the end room pulled wide and Nurse Baxter emerge at a run, her face showing shock and fear. She came hurrying towards Helen, who stepped into the corridor and barred the way.

Nurse Baxter halted as if she had run into a wall, and she half turned to look back at the end room. Helen looked in the same direction and saw Ralph Simpson coming into view, with a grim faced Russell at his back. Nurse Baxter turned to face Helen again, and she was completely astounded.

'Into the office,' Helen said quietly, and the girl made no protest but walked towards her. Helen accompanied her into the office, and Russell followed with a defiant Ralph Simpson. For a moment there was silence, and they looked at each other.

'Well, it's taken me some time to catch you, Simpson,' Russell said at length. 'I suppose you know that both you and Nurse Baxter can lose your jobs here because of this.'

'Because of what?' the porter demanded, and his fleshy face was suddenly ugly, his dark eyes filled with menace.

'We don't need to go into details,' Russell went on smoothly. 'If I make a report that you and Nurse Baxter were in that empty room together, in the dark, locked in embrace, what kind of an interpretation do you think the matron would put upon it.'

'But you won't report it,' Simpson said with a knowing smile.

'Really!' Russell stiffened a little. 'Pray tell me why I won't!'

'Because I could tell Matron that I've seen you and Sister Crandall doing the same thing in her office. You didn't even have the sense to switch out the light.'

'And how would you have seen such a thing?' Russell's voice was suddenly low pitched and tense.

'It's my job to see things around here,' Simpson said gruffly. 'Mrs Fredericks asked me specially to keep an eye on you and Sister Crandall.'

Helen gasped, and Simpson looked as if he could have bitten out his tongue. Russell stepped forward and seized the man by his shoulders, despite the fact that Simpson outweighed him considerably.

'So that's the way the wind blows, is it?' Russell demanded angrily. He shook the bigger man, and Simpson made no effort to prevent him. 'I suppose it was you who told her about Sister Crandall and I being in that village.'

'Naturally. I believe in carrying out the orders of my employer. I was asked to watch you. How else do you think I was in that

out-of-the-way place with Nurse Baxter? We
don't like that kind of thing. I was spying on
you, Doctor, and you'd better take your
hands off me or I'll tell Mrs Fredericks a lot
more than I've done so already. She's very
keen on all the gory details.'

Russell released the man very slowly, his
face showing that he was finding it difficult
to control his temper. He nodded slowly, his
eyes bright, narrowed and fierce.

'It's a good thing for you that I'd already
decided to do nothing about this incident
beyond letting you know that I knew it was
going on,' he said through his teeth. 'It will
stop, of course, and if I ever catch you up
here again during the night I'll do something about it. Don't think that anything
you've said has caused me to change my
mind. I'm thinking of the good of Foxfield
by holding my tongue. But there'd better
not be a next time. Now you'd better get out
of here, and if I catch you snooping around
I'll prove to you that acting the spy can be a
very dangerous business.'

Simpson sneered a little, and shrugged his
heavy shoulders. He glanced at Helen, and
there was a gleam in his dark eyes that sent
a pang of fear through her breast. Russell
stepped out of the doorway and Simpson

departed, without so much as a glance at the frightened Nurse Baxter standing by the desk. They all stood motionless, just listening to Simpson's receding footsteps, and Helen breathed deeply in an attempt to rid herself of the tension gripping her.

'Now, Nurse,' Russell said when silence filled the corridor. 'I want you to tell me just what has been going on.'

'Nothing, Doctor,' the girl replied hastily. 'You saw what was happening in that room, but that's all. I'm in love with Ralph, and he used to come up there to see me. We only stayed together for a short time. I used to watch the corridor in case anyone came up. We weren't doing any harm!'

'Your place is here in this office,' Helen remonstrated. 'If an emergency arose involving one of the patients you wouldn't have been in a position to render immediate help or send for aid. Have you completely forgotten your responsibilities?'

'But you and Doctor Garett are just as guilty!' the girl said.

'No.' Russell came forward a pace, his face showing anger. 'Simpson has tried that argument as a defence for what you've done here. But I'm not remaining silent because I'm afraid of the publicity that might come to us from any counter charge Simpson might lay against us. Don't make a mistake in thinking you can blackmail us into forgetting this business. It won't work. You'd better get it into your head that this is a serious business, and you'd better make sure that it doesn't happen again. Aren't you worried that you might lose your position here? You know that if you left under a cloud it might affect your nursing career?'

'Yes, Doctor!' There was meekness in the girl's tones now, and Russell nodded slowly.

'All right. Here the matter ends, but I'd better not have cause to recall it in future. You'd better be very careful from now on, Nurse.'

He turned and walked out of the office, and Helen followed him. They were silent until they had reached Helen's office, and then Russell heaved a long sigh and smiled.

'Well I think we've laid your ghosts, Helen,' he told her. 'I have a feeling that it won't happen again.'

'I'm sure it won't,' Helen responded. 'But aren't you perturbed about what Simpson said, Russell?'

'About him working for Julia on the side?' He shook his head. 'It's the sort of thing Julia would do. But could he have been the mystery man you heard her talking to in the summerhouse that time?'

'I've been thinking about that!' Helen's eyes were harsh as she considered. 'But the way Julia was talking to the man that afternoon makes me wonder. She said something about great things being planned, and that the man had much to gain from their association. What do you think she meant by that, Russell?'

'Who can tell?' He shrugged, ready to dismiss the whole affair lightly. 'Julia is like that. She dramatises everything. There's no limit to her depth, you know. I think she's capable of just about anything to get what she wants.'

'That's what I'm worried about.' Helen looked into his eyes, and saw the same kind of anxiety showing there as filled her heart. 'You're trying to convince yourself that she isn't planning something bad, Russell, but you do think there's something brewing.'

'I've been thinking that for a long time,' he admitted reluctantly. 'She said some strange things to me before I cut myself from her toils. She was always planning for the day when Joseph would be dead and she took over Foxfield. What she didn't promise me!' He smiled thinly. 'But that's neither here nor there! I must say, and I think I told you at the time, that she seemed pleased when she heard that Joseph didn't have much chance of surviving his operation. But the past month has proved us wrong. He's got such a will to live that he's succeeding, and another month should see him completely out of the wood. But Julia doesn't like that, Helen. I don't have to be told about her. I can sense things. In the past week she's changed a little, and each succeeding day finds her just a little bit more impatient. I'm beginning to think that we've got to take precautions against her. I'm recalling now that once she told me she believed in Euthanasia! It didn't have any significance at the time, but now I'm not so sure. Julia doesn't have a sympathetic chord in her make-up. She wouldn't cross the street to help anyone in any kind of trouble, and she's certainly not in love with Joseph, and has never been. I can't help thinking that she had big plans for me, as she suggested at the time, but they weren't the kind of plans I envisaged or what she led me to believe. I believe now that she was working on me to gain her own obscure aims. I think she was hoping to get me to kill her husband painlessly, to put him out of his misery!'

'Russell!' Helen was aghast, and her eyes

158

and face showed it. She saw him smile grimly, and he nodded.

'It sounds fantastic, doesn't it? But that's Julia all over! It could be my imagination, but I don't think so. There was too much said about it. It played on my mind subconsciously, and I think it was that as much as anything that made me find the necessary nerve to ask you out, in the first place, anyway. I pray to God I am wrong, Helen, but I'm going to keep a very close eye on Julia in future, just in case, and I want you to do the same around here. If Simpson is now implicated in my place then we can't be sure of Nurse Baxter. She's very much in love with Simpson, and might do anything he suggested. Put Nurse Hudson in charge of that floor now, and keep Nurse Baxter where you can watch her. You have reason enough now to make the change without arousing any suspicions. Will you do that, Helen?'

'Certainly,' she replied in gasping tones. 'Anything you say, Russell. But I can't believe all this. It just cannot be true.'

'Let's hope that you're right and I'm wrong,' he retorted. 'I would be very happy to be proved wrong. But we can't take chances, Helen. If Julia is as bad as I imagine then the sky's the limit. If we are prepared then there's a chance that not much harm will be done.'

Helen could only nod soundlessly, her mind overcome by the pictures which his words had conjured up. But she could see that he might be right, and it would be common sense to take as many precautions as possible. When he left her she sat down at her desk to try and think it all over, but her mind was seething with conjecture and puzzlement, and she could not find her usual peace of mind. But she did follow Russell's instructions, and sent Nurse Hudson up to the next floor and brought Nurse Baxter down to closer quarters. She hoped it was only her imagination, but there seemed to be an ominous note in the atmosphere for the rest of that night, and the uneasiness followed her for many days after...

Chapter Nine

Helen found a lot of the pleasure going out of her work in the days that followed. She had been badly shocked by Russell's suspicions of Julia Fredericks, and couldn't bring herself to agree with him. Every time she considered it her mind cringed from the decision she had to make. The whole thing seemed so incredible. It was the sort of thing one read about in the newspapers but never came up against. She did a lot of serious thinking when she was off duty, and her nerves were drawn tight when she reported for duty each night. She found Nurse Baxter very subdued in those ensuing days, but Ralph Simpson was defiant, and whenever she saw him there was a half-amused glint in his dark eyes.

Her life with Russell gave her great satisfaction. They were together at every available moment, and Helen found her love deepening with each passing day. Russell was most attentive, and proved himself in every way. During the long nights, Helen often found him coming down to the office to check with her, despite the fact that he was off duty, and she began to wonder if he was concerned about her or worried that something might happen to Joseph Fredericks.

Julia Fredericks showed herself little at the Home, coming in to visit her husband during the official visiting hours and departing immediately after, and Helen could not help thinking that the woman knew all the details of that incident in which Simpson and Nurse Baxter had been caught out. There was now every indication that any feelings the woman had for Russell were completely gone. For his part, Russell never spoke of her, and if she cropped up in the course of conversation he instantly changed the subject. Helen felt extremely satisfied.

With another week behind them, Helen began to look forward to her next long weekend, and as she went on duty one Monday evening she determined to talk to Russell about it. She was eager to take him to her parents' home, knowing that he was as eager to go with her. Taking over from Sister Denby, Helen made her first round of the patients, checked that the two nurses were attending to their routine chores, and then prepared for Doctor Lymann's round.

When she passed Nurse Baxter in the lower corridor she was struck by the girl's worried expression, and halted, gazing into her subordinate's face.

'What's wrong, Nurse?' she demanded.

'Wrong, Sister?' Nurse Baxter gave a little start of surprise and stared at Helen.

'You look as if you've carried all the troubles of the world on your shoulders since breakfast time,' Helen told her. 'Is

162

there anything I can help with?'

'There's nothing wrong, Sister. Just a few words between me and my boy friend.'

'Oh!' Helen smiled. 'Well that sort of thing happens all the time, doesn't it? I hope you'll soon make friends again.'

'Thank you, Sister.' The girl hesitated as she started to walk on, and Helen saw her moisten her lips. 'Sister, I've felt awful about that other night. That's one of the reasons why I've had a row with Ralph. I told him he shouldn't have spoken to Doctor Garett that way. It was very good of the doctor not to take the matter further. I want to say that I'm sorry it ever happened. If I'd listened to my own conscience it wouldn't have done. But you know what men are. They keep on and on until you agree with them. But you needn't worry. It won't happen again.'

'I know it won't, Nurse,' Helen said rather warmly. 'I quite understand how it happened. I wouldn't have known about it if Nurse Hudson hadn't been scared by that door of the end room upstairs always being open. I'm glad the matter was taken no further. You're a very good nurse, and it would have been a great pity if we'd lost you.'

'Thank you, Sister. I feel a little better now.'

Helen nodded and the girl went on about her duties. For a moment Helen felt extremely sorry about her part in the incident. Simpson had been technically correct in saying that Russell and she were as guilty. Russell had kissed her more than once when they had been on duty. She stifled a little sigh of regret and went up to the next floor. It was over and done with now, and no one else was any the wiser.

Nurse Hudson was in the office when Helen peeped through the doorway. The girl looked up with her wide, serious eyes, and smiled a greeting. Helen entered and stood by the desk.

'Everything all right?' she demanded.

'Yes, Sister.' Nurse Hudson nodded happily.

'What about all this business of doors opening by themselves?' Helen demanded, the incident still uppermost in her mind. She had not given the girl any details of what she and Russell had found in that end room. 'You were quite nervous during the latter part of our last tour of night duty. Doesn't it worry you now?'

'Not at all,' the girl replied with a sheepish smile. 'I have looked for the usual signs, but I'm happy to report that there has been nothing unusual happening. I put that last business down to my nerves. We do get a little tired towards the end of a month on night duty.'

'That's true.' Helen nodded. 'How is Mr Fredericks this evening?'

'Very well. He's making slow progress, isn't he?'

'Yes, but every inch is nothing short of a miracle,' Helen replied. 'I wouldn't have thought it possible when he first came here. The doctors thought he was going to die.'

'But he's a fighter, Sister. He's a fine man! He's beginning to talk more now, and the questions he asks about this place isn't anybody's business.'

'I'll go along and have a look at him,' Helen said softly. She glanced at her watch. 'Doctor Lymann will be coming around soon. Is everything ready for him up here?'

'Yes, Sister. Nurse Baxter was up here about half an hour ago, helping me put the finishing touches to the place. I've got it all under control.'

'Good. It's all good practice.' Helen smiled as she moved to the door. 'You're ambitious, aren't you, Nurse?'

'I am, but I didn't think I'd ever get the chance to take over up here. I asked Nurse

Baxter why she's changed places with me, and she said something about changes in the staff coming shortly. She expects to be made a Sister soon. You wouldn't be considering leaving Foxfield, would you?'

'Me?' Helen paused and looked at the girl. 'I don't think so.' She was startled, but managed to keep her face expressionless and her tones even.

'Have I said something I shouldn't?' the girl demanded, pulling a face. 'Perhaps Sister Denby is leaving. Nurse Baxter did tell me not to say anything, but if she knows something then surely you ought to.'

'Perhaps Nurse Baxter has been listening to rumours,' Helen suggested, smiling. She turned to depart, and as she walked along the corridor towards Joseph Fredericks' room her face lost its smile and she took a laboured breath. Was there still some intrigue taking place at Foxfield? She knew Sister Denby had no plans for leaving here, and the establishment carried only two Sisters. What did Nurse Baxter mean? Had Julia said something to Ralph Simpson? Had he told Nurse Baxter about the forthcoming changes?

For a moment Helen knew panic as she considered that she might be the one who was leaving. That would mean not seeing Russell, and such an eventuality was unthinkable. Then she gathered herself, knowing that she had done nothing to merit dismissal, and she would be very careful not to give Julia any reasons.

She found Joseph Fredericks awake, and he smiled when he saw her. His voice had strengthened considerably during the past weeks, and Helen smiled happily as she paused at the foot of the bed and studied his tired face.

'It won't be long before you're getting out of that bed, Mr Fredericks,' she said. 'Aren't you looking forward to the day you will be able to get back into harness?'

'I don't think I'll ever do that,' he replied slowly, and his faded blue eyes took on a wistful expression.

'Why ever not?' Helen shook her head as if the idea was out of the question. 'You've done remarkably well as it is. There is no limit for a man with your kind of will power.'

'But that is all it is, Sister. Just will power! I have nothing to back it with. I'm living on borrowed time. I just had to get well in order to see how the place is being run without my hand on the controls.'

'And are you satisfied with the way it's

going?' she demanded.

'Very satisfied. Julia is making a good job of it. Of course I had no doubts about her. She was a very capable and experienced nurse, you know.' He sighed heavily and relaxed a little. 'I'm very satisfied. I don't care what happens to me now.'

'You sound despondent this evening,' she told him in cheerful tones. 'Is there anything I can get you?'

'Nothing, thank you, Sister. I have everything I need. I have been well cared for since I arrived. I never thought I would found this place in order to come here and die. But I've started something of which I am very proud, and I hope it will go on when I'm dead. I suppose you know a great deal of what has been going on here in the past months. Julia has been engaged in finding someone to take my place here. It hasn't been an easy job. But she always did like a challenge. Which of the two doctors do you think should step into my shoes?'

'That's hardly a fair question, Mr Fredericks,' she told him with a gentle smile. 'I am biased in favour of one of them.'

'Of course!' He nodded slowly. 'Doctor Garett!' He smiled. 'Is it serious?'

'I think so!' She nodded quickly.

168

'I hope you will be very happy!' He sighed then, and glanced away, and Helen automatically straightened the bedclothes and touched his pillows.

'If you'll excuse me,' she said apologetically. 'I'm expecting Doctor Lymann shortly.'

He nodded and she departed, and there was a strange hollowness in her mind as she considered Joseph Fredericks. He had been an extremely clever surgeon, a man who gave his life to the exacting duty of helping others, and here he was in a sick bed, with no hope of returning to his vocation. Life was hard for some people, she thought remotely. It seemed that the better type of person suffered worst.

Doctor Lymann was waiting in her office when she entered, and Nurse Baxter was at the desk, looking rather ill at ease. Helen sent the girl to make tea, and then apologised to Lymann for not being ready for him. She told him of Joseph Fredericks' mood, and he nodded.

'It's sometimes the case with an illness like that,' he said. 'He has made tremendous progress, and against all laws of nature. But there's a balance, and I won't be surprised if we see a sudden and sharp decline in his condition. I have been expecting it, although

169

I haven't stressed this point to Mrs Fredericks. No need to pile the agony on her at the moment. She has more than enough to bear as it is.'

Helen nodded, and they started his round. She saw by her watch that they were a little behind schedule, and he knew it because he didn't spend as much time as usual with the patients. By the time they reached Joseph Fredericks' room they were on schedule, and after examining the patient, Lymann motioned for Helen to leave him alone with the man. She went back to her office.

Later, Lymann looked in, and he paused before going back to his quarters. Helen put down her pen and got to her feet as he came into the office.

'Keep a special eye on Mr Fredericks, Sister,' he said. 'I don't like the look of him. At the first sign of any complication you must call me.'

'Very well, Doctor. I'll look in on him every thirty minutes. I'll warn Nurse Hudson to be alert.'

'Good.' Lymann was satisfied, and he took his leave.

Helen looked at her watch, then went back to her work. Thirty minutes later she went to the upper floor and looked in at the office before going on to Joseph Fredericks' room. Nurse Hudson wasn't there, but as Helen looked into the corridor she saw the nurse coming from a patient's room. The girl hurried towards Helen when she saw her. Helen passed on the message about watching Joseph Fredericks, then went along to the man's room. She found him asleep, breathing regularly, and checked his pulse. It was a little irregular, but that was to be expected. Satisfied for the moment, she went back down to her office.

Nurse Baxter brought Helen a cup of tea, and informed her it was time they started going for their meal.

'Let Nurse Hudson go first,' Helen said, sipping the tea. 'I want you to keep an eye on Mr Fredericks. He's not too well again. Go for your meal when Nurse Hudson comes back, and then you can relieve me.'

'Very good, Sister.' Nurse Baxter turned away with a troubled expression on her face.

Helen watched the girl depart, and almost repeated her question about the girl's troubles, but she kept silent, and was thoughtful as she listened to Nurse Baxter's footsteps fading away along the corridor. She pictured Ralph Simpson's face, and didn't think he was a generous man. A girl would need all her wits about her to associate with him.

Thirty minutes later she went up to see Joseph Fredericks again, found him unchanged, and went along to the office to look in on Nurse Baxter. She paused as she reached the doorway, and stifled a yawn that took her by surprise. Blinking rapidly as a wave of tiredness assailed her, she looked into the office and reported to the girl that she had checked Joseph Fredericks.

'Nurse Hudson will be back at any moment, Sister. I'll go to the dining-room then.'

Helen nodded and withdrew, returning to her office, and as she sat down at the desk she yawned again. The small room was quite warm, with the central heating now working at full blast, and she tried to bring her report up to date, but from time to time her eyes closed without warning, and she recognised the danger signals. Unless she kept moving she might fall asleep. It happened from time to time, she had found. Nature tried to assert itself, and probably one night in a dozen would be a difficult period, with sleep trying to overtake the senses at every opportunity. She got up and walked to the window, opening it fully and taking a deep breath of the cold night air. Then she went into the corridor and made a silent round of the patients, willing herself to remain awake.

Nurse Baxter appeared after Helen had been to Joseph Fredericks' room again, and Helen handed over her responsibilities and went to the dining-hall for her meal. She felt dull-witted and very tired, and ate her meal with difficulty. Afterwards she almost fell asleep at the table, and had to use every effort she possessed to remain awake. Before going back on duty she sluiced her face in cold water, and felt a little easier as she went back to her office, but she was unsteady on her feet, and her senses seemed just a little bit out of focus.

As the night wore on Helen felt worse, and by the time Nurse Baxter brought round the second cup of tea she was finding it most difficult to keep her eyes open.

'You're looking tired, Sister,' the nurse observed. 'Are you feeling all right?'

'Yes thank you, Nurse,' Helen replied. 'Would you go and take a look at Mr Fredericks?'

'Certainly, Sister. You drink this tea. It will pull you together a bit.'

Helen took the tea and set it down on the desk. She blinked her eyes rapidly, frowning

173

as she stifled a yawn. Sipping the tea, she tried to force her mind to concentrate, but the bad feeling persisted, and she put her head in her hands and closed her eyes for a moment, feeling dizzy and unwell. Was she sickening for something? The thought crossed her mind, and she pushed herself to her feet as another spasm of tiredness overwhelmed her. Taking a turn around the desk, Helen shook her head, and staggered as her senses whirled. She drank the rest of her tea, felt a little better, and sat down at the desk to go on with her paperwork. A glance at her watch showed the time to be almost 2 a.m. She sighed and forced herself to concentrate. Her writing suddenly blurred and she shook her head. What was wrong with her? She felt alarm seep into her dazed mind, and suddenly dropped her pen and got to her feet. She took a walk along the corridor, moving briskly, trying to instil some life into her mind, but she felt heavy-minded, and acted just as if she were in a dream.

Going back into the office, she sat down again, but almost immediately her eyes began to close, and she stood up violently and paced the office. Her hands were trembling and her legs felt unsteady.

Nurse Baxter appeared, her approach silent, and when she stood in the doorway she watched Helen closely. 'Shall I go and check Mr Fredericks, Sister?'

'Yes please, Nurse.' Helen faced the girl, and saw a strange expression upon her face. 'Is anything wrong?' she demanded.

'No, Sister. I was thinking that you look rather tired.'

'I'm all right. Go and take Mr Fredericks' pulse.'

Nurse Baxter departed, and Helen sighed wearily and sat down at the desk. She put her head in her hands and closed her eyes for a moment. She kept telling herself that she mustn't fall asleep. She blinked her eyes, but kept them closed because the light in the room suddenly seemed too bright for her. The next thing she remembered was being shaken by the shoulder

'Sister Crandall, wake up!' The sentence was repeated again and again, and Helen felt her consciousness held at bay by some strange power that paralysed her mind. She tried to drop back into sleep; her whole being craved for it, but the hand at her shoulder was insistent, and the voice kept talking loudly in her ear. 'Sister Crandall, wake up!'

Helen slowly opened her eyes and stared

up into a blurred face. She blinked rapidly, and by degrees the face slipped into focus. She was surprised to see Sister Denby standing before her, grim faced and grave, and behind the Sister was Doctor Lymann. For a moment Helen stared at them in some surprise, then looked around quickly, her first thought that she was in her bedroom, but she was surprised to find herself in the office, and then it came to her with full horror. She was on duty!

'Yes, Sister!' Sister Denby spoke harshly. 'You are on duty – asleep on duty!'

Helen lifted a hand to her head and rubbed her eyes. She stifled a yawn, and there was a roaring sound in her ears. She looked up again, and Doctor Lymann stepped forward, his expression tense.

'Sister, when was the last time you checked Mr Fredericks?'

'What's the time?' Helen had trouble recollecting her scattered wits, and she stared at the dial of her watch without actually seeing it.

'It's just after three-thirty,' Lymann said sternly.

'Are you ill, Sister?' Sister Denby demanded.

'Ill? No! I felt strange for a bit, and just

176

closed my eyes. It was about two, I remember. Nurse Baxter checked Mr Fredericks at two.'

'Nurse Baxter has checked Mr Fredericks every thirty minutes for the last three hours, she informs us. She hasn't seen you since two a.m., and Nurse Hudson on the next floor reports that you have not been up there since she came back from her meal earlier.' There was a grim note in Lymann's harsh tones. 'This is a very serious matter, Sister Crandall. I have no option but to suspend you from duty until a full enquiry has been made. I don't have to tell just how serious it is, do I? In all probability you'll lose your job through this. Go to your room. Sister Denby will take over here. You'll see Matron first thing in the morning.'

Helen stared uncomprehendingly from one intent face to another, and suddenly saw Nurse Baxter standing in the doorway, watching her with a worried expression on her face. In a blinding flash of intuition she thought she saw the whole amazing truth. Those strange feelings she had experienced before falling asleep! They were consistent with being drugged! That tea Nurse Baxter had brought her! She had felt sleepy after drinking it. In an instant there was a picture

177

of Julia's face in Helen's mind, wearing a mocking expression, and the connection between the woman and the situation that now faced Helen needed no further explaining.

'Doctor,' Helen said anxiously, hardly knowing what she said. 'I demand that you examine me now. I believe I've been drugged!'

Chapter Ten

'Drugged!' There was a wealth of surprise in the doctor's voice. 'What on earth are you talking about, Sister? How can you have been drugged? Is this your defence against the charge that will be brought against you?'

'It certainly isn't an excuse,' Helen said firmly. 'Examine me now, in Sister Denby's presence. I'm saying that the tea I was given tonight had some form of drug in it.' She glanced at Nurse Baxter, and could tell by the expression on the girl's face that she was near to the truth. 'You made that tea, Nurse Baxter. What did you put in it?'

'Nothing, Sister!' The girl's face was scarlet as Lymann and Sister Denby turned to face her. 'I don't know what you mean!'

'This is a very serious charge you're making, Sister,' Lymann said. 'Are you sure you want to go on with it? Won't it be easier for you to plead guilty to the charge of falling asleep on duty?'

'No!' Helen shook her head. 'I know what I'm saying, Doctor. It probably sounds incredible to you, but if I'm to prove I'm right then it's got to be done, now, before it's too late. Will you examine me?'

'I'm not so sure that I ought,' Lymann said slowly.

Helen looked into his face, remembering what he had said about getting Joseph Fredericks' job if the surgeon died. Was Lymann in Julia's clutches as well? She took a deep breath.

'Very well,' she said. 'There is another doctor on the premises. Will you remain here, Sister?' She glanced at Sister Denby as she moved to the desk. 'I shall need an independent witness, no doubt. Nurse Baxter, come into the office and sit down. Doctor Garett will want to ask you some questions.'

The girl came into the office, showing great reluctance, and sister Denby moved impatiently.

'I just hope you know what you're doing,

Sister Crandall,' she said firmly. 'I don't know what is happening here, but if you suspect that you have been drugged then we ought to investigate. As you say, later will not do. Doctor Lymann, will you examine Sister Crandall?'

Lymann came forward slowly, his face expressionless, but he shot a glance at Nurse Baxter as he reached her.

'Is there anything in what Sister Crandall says, Nurse?' he demanded harshly.

'I don't know, Doctor. I certainly didn't put anything in her tea. If she has been drugged then it is without my knowledge.'

'I began to feel strange after the first cup of tea,' Helen said. 'Thinking back to the symptoms, they are consistent with a sleeping draught. But I had no idea that was the trouble. If I had given it thought no doubt I would have reasoned it out. Then Nurse Baxter gave me a second cup of tea, at the usual time, and it really knocked me out.'

'Sit down, Sister,' Lymann said slowly. He was clearly reluctant to examine Helen. But with Sister Denby there he could not refuse. Sister Denby moved in closer as he stood over Helen, and for a moment there was silence while Lymann examined Helen's eyes.

'She has certainly taken a drug within the past two hours,' Sister Denby said firmly, and there was some slight relaxation of her facial expression. 'Don't you agree, Doctor?' she prompted.

'Yes.' There was great reluctance in Lymann's voice, and it made Helen wonder. 'But it doesn't mitigate this serious matter. Falling asleep on duty is the worst crime in the Nursing calendar.'

'But if I'm the victim of a plot to discredit me, Doctor,' Helen said quickly, 'what then?'

'This sounds like nonsense to me,' Lymann said thinly.

'Are you suggesting that I drugged myself?' Helen countered.

'I am not suggesting anything, just trying to understand, that's all.'

'Then perhaps Nurse Baxter can throw some light on the matter,' Helen retorted. She sat up a little straighter when she saw her teacup and saucer still on the desk in front of her, and she leaned forward and seized the cup, feeling relief seeping into her breast as she did so. 'This should prove what I say,' she said, handing the cup to Sister Denby. 'Keep that safe, Sister, until the dregs can be analysed.'

Helen glanced at Nurse Baxter as she gave the all important cup to Sister Denby, and she saw consternation in the girl's eyes.

'There you are,' she said thinly. 'Just look at Nurse Baxter's face. Do you need more evidence than her expression?'

'This is ridiculous, Sister,' Lymann protested. 'What would you expect the nurse to show after making such an accusation?'

Helen reached across the desk and lifted the receiver of the telephone. There was silence in the office as she rang Russell's room. She could feel all eyes upon her, and she glanced from one intent face to another as she waited for Russell to answer.

'Hello!' Russell's voice was filled with sleepiness. 'Who's that?'

'Russell, I'm sorry to wake you, but this is urgent. Can you come down to my office immediately?'

'Helen!' His tones sharpened. 'What's wrong?'

'Nothing, if you can come at once,' she said.

'I'll be right with you.' The line went dead and Helen replaced her receiver.

Lymann moved towards the door, and Helen called to him.

'I'd rather you stayed, Doctor. Sister

Denby, will you act as a witness for me, and testify exactly to the actions of everyone here?'

'I'll certainly record the truth of what I've heard and seen,' Sister Denby said primly. 'I'm not satisfied with this myself, Sister. I can see that you have taken a drug, even if Doctor Lymann isn't prepared to swear to it. I'm concerned about it, and I shall be very interested to learn how you took the drug.' She glanced down at the cup in her hands. 'If there are traces of a drug in here then someone is going to have to reply to a series of most important questions.'

'I swear I don't know anything about this,' Nurse Baxter said wildly. 'If the drug was put into the cup then it was done without my knowledge.'

'And how would that happen?' Sister Denby demanded.

'I don't know.' There was panic in Nurse Baxter's voice, and Helen sighed gently in relief. It wouldn't be too difficult to get at the truth.

Russell arrived, a little breathless, and wearing a dressing-gown over his hastily donned clothes. He paused in the doorway of the office and stared around with some surprise, and a frown touched his brows as he let his gaze come to rest upon Helen's drawn, pale features.

'What's happening here?' he demanded.

'Sister Crandall was found asleep here in the office by Nurse Baxter,' Lymann said before anyone else could speak. She telephoned for Sister Denby, who called me, and we came down together. We found Sister Crandall asleep at the desk, and Sister Denby had some difficulty in awakening her.'

Russell's face slowly changed from enquiry to disbelief. Helen moved around the desk to his side, and together they confronted Sister Denby.

'You say you had difficulty in awakening me, Sister,' Helen said. 'Would you say I was in a normal sleep?'

'No, I would not!' Sister Denby's voice was tense and high pitched, edged with suspicion. 'I've been thinking since you said you had been drugged, Sister. I don't like this one bit, and I suggest that the police are called in. This is a very serious matter, and the complete truth should be brought to light.'

'There's no need for the police!' Lymann said quickly, glancing at Nurse Baxter, who was white-faced and shaking. 'Perhaps I was a little hasty in saying that Sister Crandall would lose her job here.'

'Lose her job!' Russell glanced quickly at Helen, who nodded slowly. Then he took a sharp breath. 'So that's it!' He smiled thinly. 'I was wondering how long it would take Julia to get around to making trouble. Lymann, I don't know how deeply you're involved in this, but I shall find out.'

'I am not involved in any way,' the doctor protested. 'I was called down here, the same as Sister Denby, because Nurse Baxter found her superior asleep on duty and couldn't wake her.'

'Couldn't wake her because she had been drugged?' Russell demanded instantly. He glanced towards Sister Denby. 'Is that the cup Helen used?'

'Yes!' Sister Denby nodded. 'I'm going to have the contents analysed.'

'Who made the tea?' Russell looked towards Nurse Baxter, and the girl seemed to squirm in her seat.

'I made it the same as always,' the girl said defiantly. 'I didn't put anything in it that would harm Sister Crandall.'

'If you didn't then who did?' Sister Denby demanded. 'Are you suggesting that Sister Crandall drugged herself just to cause all

185

this fuss?'

'No, Sister. I just don't know what happened.'

'Tell me how you make the tea,' Russell encouraged in gentle tones.

'First, Russell, will you examine me and give your opinion on my statement that I've been drugged this evening?'

'No need to examine her, Doctor,' Sister Denby said. 'Doctor Lymann did that, but couldn't say for sure. However I could see quite plainly that Sister Crandall has taken a drug since coming on duty. How she came to take it will be revealed, no doubt, when the police start asking questions.' She looked directly at Nurse Baxter. 'And there is the evidence of this cup. Does it contain traces of a drug, Nurse?'

'I wouldn't know,' Nurse Baxter said firmly, but her voice was trembling.

'This is a very serious matter,' Russell said, moving to Helen's side and looking intently into her eyes. 'The pupils are dilated. Without a doubt you've taken something in the nature of a strong sedative. Who was in charge of the sleeping draughts tonight?'

'I was,' Nurse Baxter said in a low voice.

'I see!' Russell's voice cracked across the room. 'And which of the patients on your list did not get the drug? How did it get out of your possession and into Sister Crandall's tea? Can you explain that, Nurse.'

'You're bullying her, Russell,' Lymann said. 'It won't do Sister Crandall's case any good, you know. You're known to be biased in her favour.'

'But I'm not, Doctor,' Sister Denby said. 'I'm as eager as Doctor Garett to get at the truth. Sister Crandall's whole career is in jeopardy, and who is to say that the same thing couldn't happen to me one night?' She turned and looked at Nurse Baxter. 'Was this dreadful thing done as a prank, Nurse?'

The silence that followed the question seemed to stick in Helen's throat. She knew that whatever had happened, it wasn't done as a prank. Julia Fredericks had to be behind it.

'Will you answer my question, Nurse?' Sister Denby repeated. 'I assure you the police will be called in if I don't get a satisfactory answer.'

'I suggest we all go to our rooms and forget about it until morning,' Lymann said.

'Does that mean I'm suspended from duty pending this enquiry?' Helen demanded.

Lymann shook his head. 'I said that because I didn't know about this drug business,' he said slowly. 'I thought it was a plain case of you falling asleep on duty.'

'Surely you know Sister Crandall better than that, Lymann,' Russell said thinly. 'I'm not satisfied with the way you've been trying to handle this. I am certainly not going to bed until I have the answers to some very pertinent questions. What about you, Sister Denby?'

'I agree with you, Doctor. We must get to the bottom of this. Someone is going to lose her job, and that's a fact. If it isn't Sister Crandall then it will be Nurse Baxter.'

'It isn't my fault,' Nurse Baxter wailed. 'It was done for a joke, that's all.'

'Are you admitting that you deliberately administered a drug to Sister Crandall without her knowledge?' Lymann demanded in rasping tones.

'Yes.' The word was almost inaudible, but it was sufficient to make Helen feel weak with relief.

'A joke!' Russell said thinly. 'What kind of a joke is it to drug your superior, especially working in a place where she is responsible for three dozen sick people? Oh no! You're not going to get away with it as easily as that, Nurse Baxter. If it had been a joke it wouldn't have gone any further than you and Sister Crandall. But as soon as she was unconscious you called for Sister Denby and Doctor Lymann. I would say your intentions were very far removed from a joke. You intended that Sister Crandall should lose her position here.'

'That's not true!' Nurse Baxter got to her feet.

'I can think of no other reason for your actions, Nurse,' Sister Denby said angrily. 'I think you're the one should be relieved from duty, and if I were Matron you would be leaving Foxfield as soon as possible in the morning, and you wouldn't obtain a nursing job again as long as you live.'

'There's no need to be so harsh, Sister,' Russell said slowly. 'I'm sure we can afford to be lenient if Nurse Baxter will tell us exactly what happened, and who put her up to it.'

Helen sat down at the desk again, her blue eyes steady on Nurse Baxter's face. She could see the girl's complete discomfiture, and knew a little pity for her, but the action had been potentially dangerous in several ways. An emergency involving one of the patients might easily have arisen, and with the Sister incapacitated the result could have proved fatal.

'I did it as a joke,' Nurse Baxter said. 'There was nothing else to it.'

'I'm not satisfied with that explanation,' Russell said grimly. 'If you try my patience too much, Nurse, then there will be other revelations to be made to Matron in the morning. I'm sure you wouldn't want that situation to arise.'

'What are you talking about, Russell?' Lymann demanded.

'It doesn't matter for the moment,' Russell replied. 'I want the truth from Nurse Baxter, and I'm going to get it.' He returned his attention to the girl. 'Now then, this is your last chance. If you don't tell the truth I shall ring for the police. Then everything will have to come out, and you won't be the only member of the staff to suffer instant dismissal. Are we going to clear up this matter or shall I pass on the responsibility to the right quarter?'

'I'm sorry,' Nurse Baxter said hesitantly. 'I did put the sleeping draught in Sister Crandall's tea. I put some in the first cup and the rest in the second.'

'Why?' Russell demanded. 'That's what I'm interested in, Nurse. Why did you do it?' His tones were rough, edged with impatience, and the girl flinched a little. This time

Lymann did not remonstrate with Russell, and Sister Denby leaned forward as she waited for Nurse Baxter's reply.

'I was promised the Sister's job if I could do something to get rid of her,' came the low-voiced answer.

'And who made that promise to you?' Russell cracked sharply.

'Mrs Fredericks!' Nurse Baxter hung her head in shame.

'Did she suggest the sleeping draught in Sister Crandall's tea?' Lymann demanded.

'Yes. She was a nursing Sister herself. She gave me the stuff and told me how much to use. I think I must have put in just a little too much. Sister Crandall was supposed to look as if she were sleeping normally. When I looked in at her later and saw her fast asleep I lost my nerve. I was supposed to wash out the cup, but I overlooked it. Now I've made a real mess of everything, and I'm sorry I ever agreed to do it.'

'Why did you agree?' Lymann demanded. 'Was it solely because you were promised Sister Crandall's job?'

'No. Mrs Fredericks said she would get rid of me, and Ralph Simpson as well, if I didn't do it. I had no choice. I would never have seen Ralph again if we'd both left here. I couldn't face that, so I agreed to do it.'

There was an ensuing silence, and Helen could feel her pulses pounding in her temples. She watched Nurse Baxter with pity in her eyes. But there was no expression on Russell's face as he glanced around at them.

'This is a foul mess!' he said. 'What are we going to do about it?'

'There's only one thing to do,' Sister Denby said strongly. 'Matron must have a report tomorrow morning, and I think the police should be informed.'

'I don't like the sound of that,' Lymann said slowly.

'And neither do I,' Russell said. 'But, it's really up to you, Helen? Do you want to make an official complaint about this?'

'What effect would the resulting publicity have on Foxfield?' Helen demanded. 'I suppose Mrs Fredericks could be charged for aiding and abetting Nurse Baxter. What would that do to Joseph Fredericks?'

'Those are the questions I'm asking myself,' Russell said. 'If you are ready to forget about it, Helen, then the rest of us can do no less, if only for the name of Foxfield. Apart from that, the news would kill Joseph, wouldn't it? We owe him something, and if

192

we hand over his wife to the police it will be the end of him and of us. But I'm not thinking of myself! We would get over the slurs in time. But Joseph wouldn't.'

'And Mrs Fredericks would escape punishment for what she's done,' Sister Denby said. 'I never liked her. She's not suited to the position she holds. Can't we do something about her?'

'Leave her to me,' Russell said firmly. 'In the morning I shall have a very enlightening talk with Julia.'

'And Nurse Baxter?' Lymann asked, and they all stared at the girl. 'I am of the opinion that a report of this should be made to Matron,' Lymann went on. 'But I can understand why we should keep it quiet. Because of Joseph Fredericks I am prepared to forget that I was called down here. But what of Nurse Baxter? Are you prepared to have her working with you after what has happened, Sister Crandall?'

'Yes,' Helen said without hesitation. 'If she will give us her promise not to be led astray again.'

'I promise,' Nurse Baxter said instantly. 'I wouldn't have done it but for the pressure they put on me.'

'They?' Russell questioned.

193

'Mrs Fredericks and Ralph, my boy friend,' the nurse replied.

'So he's in this.' Russell exchanged a glance with Helen. 'I think we can safely leave this to me now,' he went on. 'I can promise you that after I've finished with Julia there will be some changes around here, and for the better.'

'Then I'm going back to bed,' Lymann said. 'But I warn you, if any of this evening's business does get out then I shall provide Matron with a full story of it. What happens then will be out of all our hands. This leaves a bad taste in my mouth, and the sooner something is done to remedy the state of affairs the better.'

'So you're not one of Julia's blue-eyed boys!' Russell said softly.

'I'm ambitious, like the rest of you,' Lymann retorted, 'but I wouldn't place myself in that woman's power for anything in the world.'

'That makes my job easier,' Russell retorted. 'Julia is fast running out of candidates. I'll see to it that Ralph Simpson gets the fright he so rightly deserves.' He glanced at Sister Denby. 'I would get a report on the analysis of those tea dregs if I were you, Sister, and keep it in a safe place. If I should encounter any difficulty in proving to Julia Fredericks that her little games are at an end then we'll resort to good old-fashioned blackmail to quieten the situation.'

Lymann nodded grimly and departed, and Sister Denby followed him, taking the teacup with her. Russell looked at Helen, his face showing strain, and Helen glanced at Nurse Baxter.

'You may go back about your duties, Nurse. Check Mr Fredericks, will you?'

'Yes, Sister.' The girl moved to the door, filled with relief. There she paused and looked back at Helen. 'I'm ever so sorry, Sister,' she said. 'I didn't mean you any harm.'

'You would have started much more than you intended if you had been successful this evening,' Russell said sharply. 'It's about time you began living up to your responsibilities, Nurse. Don't forget that other business with Simpson. We're not likely to, and one more slip on your part will see you gone from here in very short order.'

The girl nodded miserably and hurried away, and Helen sighed heavily and sat down wearily behind the desk. Russell watched her for a moment, then sighed.

'I didn't think Julia would stoop to this,'

he said harshly. 'I've been under-estimating her for some time. But things will be different after this, I assure you, Helen. She's eaten up with jealousy in all things. No-one must have anything better than she, or do anything greater. It's her one all-consuming fault, and it will bring about her downfall in the end.' He came to her side and put an arm around her shoulder. 'Are you feeling all right now, dearest?' he asked in a whisper. 'Can you carry on here until morning?'

'I'll be all right, Russell,' she told him, smiling gently. 'I'll have a cup of strong coffee in a moment, then keep moving until the effects of this business wears off. But it's been quite a shock, I can tell you, and I don't think I shall ever feel easy here as long as I stay.'

'I know what you mean, and I'm going to take steps to see about the both of us getting out of here,' he retorted.

'What do you mean?' she queried.

'I mean I'll take a partnership with my father and leave, and you'll go with me,' he promised. 'Would you go with me?' he added in afterthought.

'I think I would follow you to the ends of the earth!' she replied firmly, and there was much in her blue eyes to confirm her words.

Russell bent over her and kissed her forehead. 'I'll get back to bed now,' he said. 'It's going to be a hard morning tomorrow, but somehow I'm looking forward to it. It will certainly put a curb on Julia, and that's something which should have been done a long time ago.'

Helen silently agreed, and when he had gone back to his room she got to her feet and paced the office. But despite the dramatic happenings of the night, she felt easier than she had been for weeks. At last she could really believe that anything which existed between Russell and Julia before he realized his love for her was finally over...

Chapter Eleven

Helen went off duty at the usual time next morning, and was not sorry to get into bed. She lay for a timeless period with her thoughts trying to piece together all the little scraps of knowledge and the impressions teeming through her mind. But she was eager to learn from Russell exactly what happened when he confronted Julia, and she didn't think she would sleep peacefully until some of the questions were answered. But the exertions of the night had taken their toll of her strength and nervous energy, and before she knew it she had drifted into sleep and knew no more until she awoke at her customary time.

Coming back to consciousness was like returning from a wild flight of fancy in a daydream. The moment she opened her eyes there was a rush of impressions and thoughts and questions all clamouring for the prominent places in her brain. She sat up and looked at her watch, noting the time and getting out of bed instantly. She had to see Russell and learn the new situation, for she didn't doubt that when Julia learned of the revelations of the previous night there would be hasty changes made.

The fact that she had come very close to falling victim to Julia's scheming filled Helen with anger and wonder. Why was the woman so keen to get her obscure way? What was she after that she had to pit one male member of the staff against another? Was it just her nature, or were deeper plans afoot? Helen could not forget what Russell had said about Julia. Hadn't the woman ever loved her brilliant husband? Did Julia really want Joseph Fredericks dead?

When she was dressed Helen left her room and went down to find Russell. She had no idea what he would be doing at this particular time of the afternoon. He would be off duty, she recalled, and they often met in the grounds during such afternoons, without making prior arrangements. Leaving the building, she followed the paths that weaved through the extensive grounds, and eventually arrived at the summerhouse. She paused before going close, thinking of the afternoon when she had overheard Julia talking to that unseen and unknown man. She still could not get rid of her belief that the man had been Russell, despite his denials. But jealousy had no part in her life, and she thrust the thought aside and tried to concentrate upon the more important things.

Her heart seemed to miss a beat when she spotted a man in the entrance to the summerhouse, and she saw it was Russell. She paused to study him from a distance, and loving thoughts ran through her mind in endless procession. Half hidden by some bushes, she was about to go forward and announce her presence when she saw a movement on the further side of the little building. The next moment Julia appeared, and paused in the clearing to stare at Russell.

'So this is where you spend your spare time,' the woman said loudly, and Russell started and looked around quickly. Helen saw his expression change when he recognized Julia, and for some obscure reason she felt glad at the sight of his distaste.

'I'm waiting for my future wife,' Russell said strongly, and Helen gasped as the import of his words struck home in her.

'She can't do anything for you, Russell,' Julia said smoothly. 'Why do you have to be such a fool and throw yourself away on her? I gave you great chances. What's wrong with me?'

'Nothing, as far as I'm concerned. All I have against you is your lack of scruples, plus the fact that I don't love you, and I never did. We're totally different in everything, Julia, and apart from that, you're a married woman.'

'I understand that my husband hasn't long to live,' Julia said.

'Then you've been misinformed. From my examinations I would say he has a great number of years yet left to him. I don't know what Lymann has been telling you, but he's lying when he says Joseph hasn't much longer. Have you been trying to buy Lymann's services?'

'I don't know what you mean!' Julia's face was livid with anger. 'How dare you talk to me like that? Perhaps I had it coming this morning. I admit I rather lost sight of the main points. But I had to do something to get rid of Sister Crandall.'

'Do you think that would have made any difference to us?' Russell demanded savagely. 'You don't know what true love is, do you, Julia?' He shook his head as he smiled gently. 'I pity you. There's not an honest emotion in you. I don't know what you hope to gain from your plans. Nothing is going to happen to Joseph. As long as I'm here you daren't do anything to shorten his life. I know you've been working on Lymann since I cut myself free from you. And there's Ralph Simpson. You've even got to work on the porter because he's a man. Your little scheme almost worked, too, didn't it?' Russell shook his head wearily. 'Go on and leave me alone, Julia. The very sight of you makes me ill.'

'You fool!' the woman hissed, and Helen was startled to see the terrible expression which came to Julia's face. 'I gave you the finest chance you'll ever have, but you tossed it back into my face because you fell in love. Well I don't need you. This morning you threatened to resign and leave here, and I pleaded with you to stay just a while longer. But I can see that I'll be wasting my time with you. All right, I accept your resignation. You'll be free to leave in a month, and perhaps you'll be good enough to put it in writing to make it official.'

'With the greatest pleasure,' Russell said, smiling thinly. 'You can expect a resignation from Sister Crandall. Last night you pulled the lowest trick I've ever heard of in an attempt to discredit her. You don't know how lucky you are to escape prosecution. But your lesson will come home to you one day, Julia, and I hope you will remember my words.'

Julia turned haughtily and began to stride away, but Russell called to her.

'Just hear me out,' he said sharply. 'I didn't even guess at the time what you were endeavouring to get me to do. But I know it well enough now, and I warn you, Julia, that if anything happens to Joseph that doesn't appear to be natural then I'll raise enough smoke to drive the truth out of you.'

Helen listened with a frown on her face, and her mind was beset by what Russell said. She watched Julia turn and storm away, and she suppressed a shiver as Russell stepped back into the summerhouse and sat down in the gloom of a corner. Moving away, Helen hurried along a path, then cut across in another direction to approach from the house. She walked up to the summerhouse and peered inside, and Russell called cheerily to her.

'I've been waiting some time for you to appear, Helen. Come on in. It looks as if it's going to rain at any moment. Do you want to go for a drive or would you rather sit and talk about the future?'

'I'd rather talk about the future,' she said without hesitation, and entered the little building and sat down at his side. His face was calm now, and a little pale, she noticed.

'Did you see Julia on your way here?' he demanded tensely.

'No. Has she been here?'

'Came up a few moments ago. But it doesn't matter about her. No doubt you're impatient to learn what was said this morning. I gave it to her hot and thick, and she didn't like it. I brought it all out, and left nothing untouched. You needn't worry about her again as long as you're here.' He broke off and sighed heavily. 'I have done something which may prove a little foolish, Helen.'

'Never,' she said with a smile, forcing away her own tensions in order to appear care-free.

'I've given a month's notice.' His face was showing great determination. 'It's not according to the rules of the contract I hold with Joseph, but the circumstances warrant a breach of contract, and Julia wouldn't dare contest it. Not only that, but I have told her that you'll be leaving with me.' He looked at her, his face showing anxiety. 'I know I have a nerve for doing so, but I'm sure you won't want to stay on here after I'm gone, will you?'

'I wouldn't dare stay on without your pro-tection, Russell,' she told him, and he slid an arm around her shoulders and leaned sideways to kiss her.

'My dearest Helen! How glad I am that we've come together. It would have been a tragedy if anything prevented this moment. I shan't be happy now until we're both well away from this place. To think that I used to cherish this job! Happiness is a frame of mind, isn't it? I couldn't visualize being in any other job at any other place, but that was before I realized that I'm in love with you. Since making the big discovery I've found the true values, and it doesn't matter what I do in future or where I'll be, so long as you're there with me, Helen.'

She was touched by his words, and tears of happiness glinted in her blue eyes. He smiled as he saw her emotion, and put his arms around her, kissing her passionately.

'Helen,' he said softly, 'You'll never know how much you've done for me. I was a doctor in bondage, and I didn't realize it until you made me love you. I was completely in Julia's clutches, and I'm sure I would have done anything she asked if you hadn't saved me, made me realize in time what it was that I had to lose.' He laughed harshly. 'I stood to lose everything, and Julia so had me in her power that I was believing that she could be my salvation!'

'Russell, what is it Julia wanted you to do?' There was an urgency in her tones that drew his gaze, and he smiled slowly and patted her hand.

'If I knew that definitely, Helen, I would have informed the police,' he said grimly. 'But all I have to go on are a number of veiled hints. Whether she's gone any further with these other men she's working on I don't know, but while I'm here I shall keep a close eye on what's happening.'

'And after we leave?' she said. 'You can't

say it isn't any of our business after we leave because neither of us is made like that. You think Julia intends doing away with her husband, don't you?'

'I've had that dreadful thought for a long time now,' he admitted. He sighed heavily. 'I don't know what I'm going to do at the end of the month. I know I can't just walk out and wipe it all from my mind. It would be with me for the rest of my life.'

'This is terrible,' Helen said helplessly. 'Is there nothing that Julia wouldn't do to get what she wants?'

'She's been waiting to see if Joseph would die soon,' Russell said slowly. 'By all reports he ought to have died within a fortnight of his operation, but he's been hanging on, and gaining ground. He looks like hanging on for a long time yet. Lymann has been telling lies to Julia about her husband's condition, urging her to wait in the hope of staying her hand completely. He knew all about that attempt to discredit you last night. Julia admitted as much this morning. I feel sorry for him if he's under Julia's thumb, as I think he is. But he hasn't the nerve to do what she wants. He wouldn't dare, and Julia doesn't know that. She's made a wrong assessment of Lymann's courage and nerve.

I can see that, but thank heaven Julia can't.'

'What is it she wants done exactly?' Helen demanded.

'Mercy killing! She knows we all owe a great loyalty to Joseph. He's suffered a lot, Helen, and I wish there was something I could do for him. It would be easy to forget one's duty under the pressures that Julia can exert. But thank God I'm out of the wood, and I'll see to it that Lymann is before we leave.' He made an impatient gesture. 'Let's forget all about this situation for a moment. I want to talk about us, Helen.'

'All right.' She smiled. 'Let us talk about us. What happens to me when we leave here? I shall have to work, Russell.'

'I shall keep you pretty busy,' he retorted cheerfully. 'Come on, do as I tell you. Forget about this place for a moment. Smile! Give me a nice big smile!'

Helen smiled, and although her every inclination was to talk about their future happiness she could not get her mind from the dreadful knowledge that Julia was indeed as bad, if not worse, than she had imagined.

But the next day or two brought anti-climax to Helen's mind. She handed in her resignation, as did Russell, and there was a lot of speculation when the news leaked out. Nurse Baxter seemed a little easier in her own mind, and Helen had no doubt the girl entertained ideas about stepping into her shoes at the end of a month. But knowing Julia, Helen doubted that Nurse Baxter's hopes would be realized. The girl had failed in her task, and failure had no hope against Julia's mania for success.

Then Joseph Fredericks had a relapse, and Helen came on duty that night to find a crisis on her hands. Doctor Lymann was on duty, and he had a nurse by the bedside. Helen took one look at the doctor's stern face and expected the worst.

'Call me as soon as there's any change in his condition, Sister,' Lymann said. 'But I don't expect him to live through the night.'

Helen nodded, and went up to the old man's room, to find him breathing harshly, his eyes closed and his face ashen. Nurse Hudson was at the bedside.

'He's dying,' the girl said. 'He won't last till morning, will he, Sister?'

'He's not expected to,' Helen replied stiffly, and there was a thought of Julia in her mind. This was what the woman wanted! At last her wishes were coming true! But Helen felt upset by the knowledge that such a dreadful desire could find gratification. She was downcast as she went on about her duties.

With Nurse Hudson at the bedside, Nurse Baxter had to return to the upper floor, and Helen handled the lower floor alone. She was kept busy until almost midnight, and had just returned to her office when Russell appeared in the doorway.

'Hello!' she exclaimed. 'Unless I'm very much mistaken, you're up rather late.'

'I've been talking to Julia,' he replied tiredly. 'She's happy at last. I examined Joseph this afternoon, and I don't think he has much longer. But I can't rest, Helen, just in case something happens to him that shouldn't.'

'But Nurse Hudson is at his bedside,' Helen said. 'Surely Julia can wait now for Nature to take its course.'

'What happens when Nurse Hudson has to go for her meal?' Russell demanded. He glanced at his watch. 'That will be very shortly, won't it?'

'I planned to bring Nurse Baxter down here and to take over myself.'

'I ought to have known you would have worked something out,' he said. 'But if you're up there and get a call from one of the patients the room will be unattended. I think I'll stay with you until Nurse Hudson gets back.'

'Would you like some coffee?' she asked.

'Can you guarantee it to be free of drugs?' he demanded.

'I'll make it myself.' She smiled a little, and then shook her head. 'I shall be glad to get away from here now, Russell. These past days have seemed like a nightmare. I feel so unsettled.'

'It's all my fault,' he replied gloomily. 'If I had stayed out of your life none of this would have happened to you.'

'I'm not complaining,' she protested. 'When this present crisis is over I shall be the happiest girl in the world.'

'Well it is almost over. I don't suppose Julia will keep any of the promises she made to anyone here. Once she gets what she wants there will be a great many changes here. I'm glad we're getting out. Next weekend we'll go home to my parents, Helen, and you'll be able to see what the situation is there. I'm sure you'll be very happy with me.'

'I know I shall.' Helen glanced at her watch. 'I'd better go up and relieve Nurse Hudson now, Russell.'

They walked to the upper floor together,

and Nurse Baxter was a little surprised to be ordered down below. She went, and Helen went along to Joseph Frederick's room. When she entered she found Nurse Hudson coming towards the door. The girl looked relieved to see her.

'I was just coming for you, Sister,' she said. 'I think Mr Fredericks is dying.'

'Fetch Doctor Garett,' Helen said quickly. 'He's in the office along the corridor. Then ring for Doctor Lymann.'

The nurse nodded and hurried off, and Helen went to the bedside and looked down at the unconscious man. She checked his pulse, finding it very weak, and he was having difficulty in breathing.

Russell came silently into the room, examined Joseph, and met Helen's glance. He nodded slowly. 'I'd better get Julia up here,' he said. 'Lymann will be here presently, Helen.'

She nodded and he departed, and silence closed in around her as she waited. A few moments later Ellis Lymann entered the room. His face was grave. When he had made an examination of the unconscious man he sighed and shook his head.

'Doctor Garett has gone for Mrs Fredericks,' Helen said.

'I know.' Lymann was tense. He looked at Helen with direct gaze, and nodded slowly. 'She'll be happy about this! I want you to know, Sister, that I'm leaving here as soon as a replacement can be found. I'm not proud of some of the thoughts I've had here. That woman could charm the Devil!' He sighed again and began to pace the room.

Helen remained in the room until the door opened and Julia entered. Russell was behind her, and he stood beside Helen while Julia went to the bedside. The woman's face was grave, but showed no expression.

'Has he regained consciousness at all?' Julia demanded.

'No,' Helen said, and they watched Julia take her husband's pulse.

'He's a lot weaker,' Julia commented. 'Can you bring him to, Doctor, before he dies?'

'No,' Lymann said harshly. 'He's already gone from you, Julia.'

She didn't like the sound of his voice, and glanced quickly at Helen and Russell.

'You're not on duty, Doctor Garett,' she said thinly, 'and you don't have to remain, Sister. Doctor Lymann will call you if you're needed.'

'Stay here, Sister,' Lymann said. 'You're under my instructions while we're both on

212

duty. I'd appreciate it if you would remain, Russell.'

'Certainly,' Russell said, and moved to a chair and sat down. He watched Julia impassively, and Helen saw the raw hatred that showed in the woman's face. But after some moments Russell got to his feet. 'Your nurses should start getting away to their meal,' he said to Helen. 'I'll go and relieve Nurse Hudson for you.'

'Wait a moment,' Lymann said. He was standing by the bedside, his attention upon the patient, and he suddenly bent over the bed and placed a hand upon Joseph Frederick's chest. Helen felt a pang stab through her, and she tightened her lips as Lymann adjusted his stethoscope and listened intently for a heartbeat. Russell moved forward slowly, and then Lymann raised his head and put away his stethoscope. 'You can all relax now,' he said gravely. 'He's dead. Perhaps you'd care to confirm, Russell.'

Helen was watching Julia's face as Russell did so, and when Russell agreed Julia gave a long, shuddering sigh and turned away. She moved to the door, and Helen was startled when Lymann called to the woman. He had covered Joseph's face, and now he faced Julia as she turned in the doorway.

'Not so fast, Julia,' he said. 'I have something to say to you.'

'Then come down to my office,' the woman retorted.

'No. I would prefer to say it here. I don't have to tell Russell about you. He found out before I did. Sister Crandall also has a good insight into your character.'

'I'm not staying to listen to insults,' Julia said angrily.

'I'm not insulting you, merely telling the truth.' Lymann smiled thinly, and Helen wondered what he had to say. 'You ought to know, Julia, that Joseph also knew all about you. I'm sure you thought you had concealed your true nature from him, but you were wrong. He used to ask me questions about your doings, and I told him. He knew when Russell came to his senses, and I told him you were amusing yourself with the porter, Simpson. I told him what plans you had for Foxfield when he was dead, and he put a stop to that by altering his will. I just want you to know that all your plans and schemes have been a waste of time. Foxfield will never fall into your clutches.'

Julia stared at him as if she had been paralysed, and her eyes were momentarily blank. Then she quivered and her expression broke. Helen was amazed at the rage which showed in the woman's face.

'You're lying!' There was contempt in her tones. 'You haven't the nerve for anything, Ellis! You were too afraid to help me, and you have no room to talk. So long as you thought there was a future here at Foxfield for you I could lead you up the garden path. You're no better than I am, or anyone else working here for that matter. I could get at them all, and with the greatest of ease.'

'Except Sister Crandall,' Lymann said thinly. 'What you tried to do to her was bad even for you, Julia. That's what really decided me! I'm following Russell's lead. Tomorrow morning there will be my letter of resignation on your desk. I want to get out. You'd better make the most of your position until the contents of Joseph's will are known. I assure you he's made other plans for the dream of his life. He wouldn't let you get your hands upon it.'

Julia stared at him for a moment, then glanced at Helen and Russell. There was a mixture of emotions showing in her tense face. Then she turned on her heel and stormed away, and Helen could hear the sound of her footsteps all along the corridor. When silence returned Lymann gave a little sigh.

'I'm sorry about that, but I had to let her know about it here in this very room, in the presence of the body of this man she hated.'

'Hated!' Helen said in barely a whisper. 'I could see she had no love for him, but surely she didn't hate him!'

'She hasn't the capacity for loving anyone,' Russell said. 'People are only to be used, as far as Julia is concerned. But I am relieved to hear that Foxfield will escape her. Joseph's dreams deserve better treatment than Julia would mete out.'

Helen moved to the door, wanting to get from the room. She started nervously as someone moved in behind her, and glanced over her shoulder to see Ralph Simpson standing there.

'I just heard he's dead,' the porter said, his fleshy face grim. 'Mrs Fredericks just passed me on the stairs, and she told me I'm fired!'

'I wouldn't pay too much attention to Mrs Fredericks,' Lymann said, uttering a short laugh. 'She'll be leaving here herself in the very near future.'

'Were you telling the truth about Joseph?' Russell demanded.

'Every word of it is true,' Lymann said. 'I feel that I've managed to put right a little of the wrongs I've done in the past few weeks. I feel unclean inside, and that comes from just knowing Julia.'

Helen walked with Russell along the corridor, and she forced her mind back to routine. Nurse Hudson went off to get her meal, and Russell went back to his room, walking with Ellis Lymann. It seemed to Helen that the whole affair was over. Joseph Fredericks was dead, and with him went the tensions and the fears. It was a tragedy that the man's noble endeavours should have aroused such bad ripples, but the source from which those ripples came was basically at fault, and Helen found herself wondering what Julia would do now! The woman had counted upon becoming the mistress of Foxfield, but the complexity of her schemes had beaten her in the end...

The night seemed long in passing. The two nurses were tense and nervous, and Helen felt moved by the events which had taken place. Each little incident had added its own burden to her soul. She made her usual rounds, and during the early hours she passed along the ground floor corridor, lost in thought, her mind working on what might have been had Russell been unable to break away from Julia's power. She was ascending the stairs again when she paused and sniffed, and her awareness was alerted. She realized that something had troubled her from the moment she reached the ground floor, but she had been too intent to notice. Now it came to her. There were tendrils of smoke drifting along the corridor, and the acrid smell of it had been trying to warn her that something was wrong!

For a moment she stood helpless in shock. Then she hurried back to the corridor and ran towards the door of Julia's office, where the smoke was thickest. She could see smoke puffing out from under the heavy door, and her heart seemed to fail her as she heard the sound of crackling flames inside the room. Her good sense deserted her and she tried to open the door. Fortunately it was locked, and she broke free from her shock and hurried along to Matron's room, seeking the nearest telephone. She dialled for the emergency services, gave the necessary details, then hurried away to arouse the staff.

Russell appeared quickly, in his dressing-gown and slippers, and Lymann followed closely. Ralph Simpson came along the corridor, his face showing shock, his hair ruffled and wild.

'I daren't open the door of the room or the fire will spread,' he said. 'But I went outside to peer through the windows. The fire has a good hold on the room. If the Brigade gets here quickly they may be able to prevent it spreading.'

'We'd better get some of the patients out of this wing,' Russell said. 'Move the less serious cases first. Ellis, take the nurses to help you.'

Lymann moved away, followed by the nurses. Sister Denby came up at that moment, followed by the other two off-duty nurses. The same expression of shock was upon all their faces.

'Get some of the patients out of the immediate area of the fire,' Russell ordered. 'Remember the fire drill that we've practised.'

'I've looked for Mrs Fredericks, but she isn't in her room,' Sister Denby said. 'Her bed hasn't been slept in.'

Helen felt a pang stab through her, and she saw the same emotion strike at Russell.

'Can she be in that office?' he demanded. For a moment they looked at one another. Then Simpson turned and started down the stairs. 'Wait,' Russell shouted, and the porter halted. Russell walked slowly towards him. 'We must think of the patients,' he said in stilted tones. 'If we open that office door the fire will explode and engulf the whole house. We'll never be able to get all the patients out!'

Helen agreed instantly, and Simpson nodded slowly. If Julia was in that room! The same thought struck all of them before they hurried to attend to the patients.

The fire brigade arrived minutes later, followed by the police. Fire was beginning to break out of the room. The fight to contain it was begun only just in time. With the good supply of water at their command, the firemen attacked relentlessly. Helen went to help with the patients, and by the time they had removed all those in immediate danger the threat to the whole building was past. The patients were transferred to another wing of the house, and there was much to be done to make them comfortable.

Russell appeared later, and dawn was beginning to show outside the windows. He sought out Helen, and found her checking the patients in their new locations.

'Julia?' Helen demanded the instant she saw him.

'She was in that room, Helen. The fireman took her body out.'

'Her body!' Helen's voice faltered. 'Then she's dead!'

'She's dead!' He nodded slowly. 'She intended to be dead. She took poison, Helen.'

'The fire?' Helen demanded.

'Julia started it.' He nodded slowly as comprehension seeped into Helen's shocked mind. 'That's the kind of woman she was. She intended that no one would have Foxfield if she couldn't. I don't suppose she ever gave a thought to the patients and staff in the house.'

Helen closed her eyes and swayed a little, and Russell put his arms around her shoulders. His nearness comforted her.

'Don't worry, Helen,' Russell said quietly. 'The house is saved. Only that office is badly damaged. Julia died in that room, and the fire has purged the house of her evil influence. It will make Joseph's soul rest easy, I'm sure. Look ahead to the future, my dearest. In three weeks we shall be leaving here. I shall work in partnership with my father. Everything will work out right, you'll see.'

'And what shall I do?' Helen demanded. 'I shall be in a strange place with a living to make.'

'But we settled all that, didn't we?' he

demanded, smiling down into her face. 'We're going to be married! Don't tell me that I overlooked asking you!' His tones softened then, and he took her chin in his hand. 'Will you marry me?' he demanded. 'It is better to get all the details settled now that we're talking them up. Do you love me enough to want to marry me?'

'Yes!' she whispered, and the light in her blue eyes emphasized the word.

He kissed her then, and she could smell smoke in his clothes. But it was the most wonderful moment of her life, and she vowed that she would never forget it. He held her close in his arms, and she could see across his shoulder, and looked through the window at the faint glow in the sky where the Autumn sun was about to break through. A new day was dawning, and with it came a whole stream of new hopes. It was a time for hope and happiness, and the tensions fell away from her mind as she realized that the night, and the shadows, were behind her...

This Large Print Book, for people
who cannot read normal print,
is published under the auspices of

ON

ok.
se

y

1	21	41	61	81	101	121	141	161	181
2	22	42	62	82	102	122	142	162	182
3	23	43	63	83	103	123	143	163	183
4	24	44	64	84	104	124	144	164	184
5	25	45	65	85	105	125	145	165	185
6	26	46	66	86	106	126	146	166	186
7	27	47	67	87	107	127	147	167	187
8	28	48	68	88	108	128	148	168	188
9	29	49	69	89	109	129	149	169	189
10	30	50	70	90	110	130	150	170	190
11	31	51	71	91	111	131	151	171	191
12	32	52	72	92	112	132	152	172	192
13	33	53	73	93	113	133	153	173	193
14	34	54	74	94	114	134	154	174	194
15	35	55	75	95	115	135	155	175	195
16	36	56	76	96	116	136	156	176	196
17	37	57	77	97	117	137	157	177	197
18	38	58	78	98	118	138	158	178	198
19	39	59	79	99	119	139	159	179	199
20	40	60	80	100	120	140	160	180	200

201	221	241	261	281	301	321	341	361	381
202	222	242	262	282	302	322	342	362	382
203	223	243	263	283	303	323	343	363	383
204	224	244	264	284	304	324	344	364	384
205	225	245	265	285	305	325	345	365	385
206	226	246	266	286	306	326	346	366	386
207	227	247	267	287	307	327	347	367	387
208	228	248	268	288	308	328	348	368	388
209	229	249	269	289	309	329	349	369	389
210	230	250	270	290	310	330	350	370	390
211	231	251	271	291	311	331	351	371	391
212	232	252	272	292	312	332	352	372	392
213	233	253	273	293	313	333	353	373	393
214	234	254	274	294	314	334	354	374	394
215	235	255	275	295	315	335	355	375	395
216	236	256	276	296	316	336	356	376	396
217	237	257	277	297	317	337	357	377	397
218	238	258	278	298	318	338	358	378	398
219	239	259	279	299	319	339	359	379	399
220	240	260	280	300	320	340	360	380	400

'
or
ıs
y